"It's my job to protect you, and I need to think about work. Not about kissing you."

"You...want...to...kiss me?"

Remorse and pain knotted in his gut. Damn it. He was a professional. He knew better than to let himself become emotionally involved while on a mission. It was bad enough he'd let himself become distracted, but his actions had crossed the line.

"I want you, Princess. Believe me when I tell you that right now I can think of only one thing—making love to you." Hunter dug his fingers into his bunched thighs, determined not to budge, wishing she'd go before he made a move he'd regret.

"I'm not a coward. You don't scare me. Despite what you say, you wouldn't force yourself on an unwilling woman."

"True. But we both know that you're *not* unwilling."

Dear Harlequin Intrigue Reader,

We've got what you need to start the holiday season with a *bang*. Starting things off is RITA® Award-winning author Gayle Wilson. Gayle returns to Harlequin Intrigue with a spin-off of her hugely popular MEN OF MYSTERY series. Same sexy heroes, same drama and danger...but with a new name! Look for *Rafe Sinclair's Revenge* under the PHOENIX BROTHERHOOD banner.

You can return to the royal kingdom of Vashmira in *Royal Ransom* by Susan Kearney, which is the second book in her trilogy THE CROWN AFFAIR. This time an American goes undercover to protect the princess. But will his heart be exposed in the process?

B.J. Daniels takes you to Montana to encounter one very tough lady who's about to meet her match in a mate. Only thing...can he avoid the deadly fate of her previous beaux? Find out in *Premeditated Marriage*.

Winding up the complete package, we have a dramatic story about a widow and her child who become targets of a killer, and only the top cop can keep them out of harm's way. Linda O. Johnston pens an emotionally charged story of crime and compassion in *Tommy's Mom*.

Make sure you pick up all four, and please let us know what you think of our brand of breathtaking romantic suspense.

Enjoy!

Sincerely,

Denise O'Sullivan
Associate Senior Editor
Harlequin Intrigue

ROYAL RANSOM
SUSAN KEARNEY

HARLEQUIN®

TORONTO • NEW YORK • LONDON
AMSTERDAM • PARIS • SYDNEY • HAMBURG
STOCKHOLM • ATHENS • TOKYO • MILAN • MADRID
PRAGUE • WARSAW • BUDAPEST • AUCKLAND

ISBN 0-373-22686-1

ROYAL RANSOM

Copyright © 2002 by Hair Express Inc.

Visit us at www.eHarlequin.com

Printed in U.S.A.

ABOUT THE AUTHOR

Susan Kearney used to set herself on fire four times a day. Now she does something really hot—she writes romantic suspense. While she no longer performs her signature fire dive (she's taken up figure skating), she never runs out of ideas for characters and plots. A business graduate of the University of Michigan, Susan is working on her next novel and writes full-time. She resides in a small town outside Tampa, Florida, with her husband and children and a spoiled Boston terrier. Visit her at http://www.SusanKearney.com.

Books by Susan Kearney

Don't miss any of our special offers. Write to us at the following address for information on our newest releases.

Harlequin Reader Service
U.S.: 3010 Walden Ave., P.O. Box 1325, Buffalo, NY 14269
Canadian: P.O. Box 609, Fort Erie, Ont. L2A 5X3

THE ZAREDS

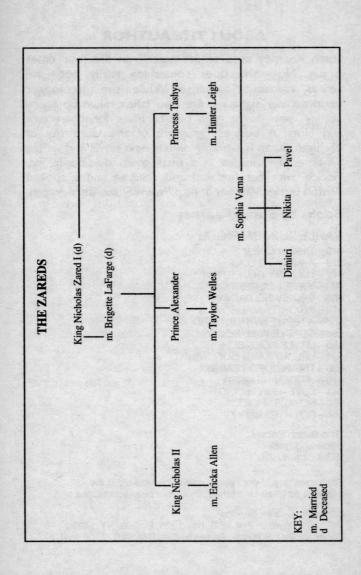

King Nicholas Zared I (d)
m. Brigette LaFarge (d)

King Nicholas II
m. Ericka Allen

Prince Alexander
m. Taylor Welles

Princess Tashya
m. Hunter Leigh

m. Sophia Varna

Dimitri   Nikita   Pavel

KEY:
m. Married
d Deceased

CAST OF CHARACTERS

Princess Tashya Zared—An independent woman in a country run by men. When her little brothers are kidnapped, she puts her life—and heart—on the line.

Hunter Leigh—A highly trained CIA operative, he has no problem impersonating a prince, but the true test comes when he tries to resist the beautiful Vashmiran princess.

Prince Alexander Zared—He's been sent away and an American agent put in his place until the traitor in their midst has been caught.

Sophia Varna Zared—Is the princess's stepmother intent on stealing the throne for her own sons?

General Levsky Vladimir—He has the Vashmiran military in the palm of his hand, but is his loyalty to the crown?

Major Stephan Cheslav—Could the general's second-in-command and Sophia's close friend be plotting to overthrow the royal family?

Ira Hanuck—Who better to carry out an assassination attempt than the chief of palace security?

For Dawn and Bryan

Prologue

"Have you ever seen such a radiant bride?" Prince Alexander Zared asked his sister, Princess Tashya.

With an approving smile, Tashya watched her oldest brother, Nicholas, King of Vashmira, and Ericka, his queen, stroll down the steps of the National Cathedral, where his coronation ceremony and their marriage had just taken place. Triumphant trumpet fanfares accompanied their footsteps, and thousands of gardenias scented the air as television cameras broadcast the event live to the world.

"Careful, Alexander. If Nicholas catches you so much as sneaking a lingering look at his wife, he'll make you ambassador to Antarctica."

Not the least perturbed, Alexander grinned. "So you've noticed our dear brother's a bit overprotective of his new bride?"

"He's so in love." Tashya could see the deep emotions in Nicholas's eyes every time he looked at Ericka. She wondered if a man would ever stare at her with such adoration, and if she'd ever respond with the open look of love she saw on Ericka's face. Good for them, Tashya thought. Nicholas deserved some happiness.

Ever since their father's assassination a year ago, Nicholas had taken on much responsibility. Stepping into their father's shoes couldn't have been easy for him. At first he had balked at accepting an arranged marriage to a stranger, but Vashmiran law had clearly stated that Nicholas must choose a bride before his coronation ceremony. Although Nicholas and Ericka had only met this past month, Tashya suspected Nicholas couldn't have chosen better on his own. Without an arranged marriage, he might never have found a wife at all. In fact, before he'd met Ericka, Tashya's more serious brother had tendencies toward being a workaholic.

However, Nicholas had lucked out and fallen in love with the American. Tashya fully approved—not that anyone had asked her approval. But she genuinely liked her independent sister-in-law and realized Ericka could help the cause. Tashya intended to seek Queen Ericka's help to establish more equality for women in Vashmira. But that would come later, after the honeymoon. Right now, as the royal couple waved to crowds of well-wishers, having the queen at his side was bringing a gentle light of satisfaction to Nicholas's eyes.

Tashya wondered if Alex would ever look so happy.

Freed from the pressure of ruling Vashmira, Alexander seemed to drift from woman to woman and party to party. Tall, dark and restless, her brother shifted impatiently from foot to foot, his attention lighting on first a pretty Muslim woman dressed in traditional clothing, then a young Jewish lady wearing a Star of David necklace. Eventually he locked gazes with a sophisticated woman sending out unmistakably lustful signals.

Tashya refrained from rolling her eyes. With her luck, the paparazzi would catch her making a face, and she would do nothing to spoil the king's wedding day. Today was going to be perfect.

She discretely elbowed Alexander in his side. "Perhaps if you stayed with one woman long enough to learn her name, you, too, might fall in love."

Alexander shrugged, his broad shoulders filling out his elegant dress uniform in a way that was sure to increase his already enormous popularity with the ladies. In fact, there had been such wild speculation over who would accompany him to the wedding that he'd chosen to go with his sister, as he often did for official functions.

For her part, Tashya always welcomed her brother's company, especially since his presence protected her from those men who couldn't see past her title to a living, breathing woman. Sure, she held a title, but that didn't mean she didn't yearn for what other women wanted—a man who loved her for her unique individuality.

Alexander winked at a set of twins, brother and sister, who couldn't be more than four. "I'll never marry."

"Why not?" Tashya waved to the crowd as the bride and groom climbed into a horse-drawn carriage. It took a few minutes for Ericka's attendants to gather and tuck her long train around her feet. With an official handshake, Nicholas thanked each of the young boys accompanying the couple. To each of the little girls, he handed a long-stemmed red rose.

"I like variety. Perhaps the flaw is mine." Alexander's gaze focused on a lovely young woman in the crowd. "I'm distracted so easily."

Tashya nudged him again. "Stop that. She's too young for you."

"I only smiled at her," Alexander said pleasantly, not the least bothered by his sister's tone of disapproval. Alexander's problem was that he expected every woman to love him, and they invariably did. It irked Tashya that while he was never alone, he often seemed lonely. "I may be the perennial bachelor but at least I go out. It wouldn't hurt you to be a little more open to the possibilities," he chided.

"Oh, right. In case you haven't noticed, we still have a double standard in this country. Our people would not accept their princess acting like their prince and going to bed with every—"

"You needn't draw me a mental picture." Alexander had the grace to wince and quickly changed the subject. "Whatever happened between you and the prince of Moldova?"

"The Toad?" Tashya shuddered, then waved again before she and Alex finally headed down the steps toward the carriage that awaited. "Absolutely nothing happened between us—that was the problem."

"The man must be blind."

"Oh, he found me attractive enough, all right. In fact, I suspect that's all he wanted. Something pretty to hang on his arm and his every word. Besides, he had horse breath. Actually, my horses have breath much sweeter than His Royal High—"

"Okay. Okay. Keep your voice down before you start another international incident."

"Nicholas's secretary of state smoothed things over."

"The prince must have been disappointed."

"Surely you don't believe I should have married a man I thoroughly disliked, so Vashmira would make an alliance?"

"Nicholas and I hoped you'd be happy with the Moldovan crown prince. I'm sorry things didn't work out."

Alexander helped her into the carriage. They would parade through the crowds and the city until they reached the palace and the grand reception hall where dignitaries and guests from around the world waited. Vashmira's palace had never looked better and the aromas wafting from the kitchens this morning had been heavenly.

Alexander pulled up his trousers slightly to avoid creases at the knees before he sat next to her on the leather seat. Naturally he'd want to look good for the legions of women he'd dance with at the ball. She, too, expected to have plenty of partners, but the evening had no appeal for her. She couldn't help worrying over the logistical nightmare of security.

Just last week Nicholas and Ericka had rooted out a traitor in their midst. The American government had responded by sending over a Secret Service team to guard the royal couple.

Along the parade route, handlers released doves from cages, and the birds soared into the sky—a sky where dark clouds threatened to block the sun. Tashya leaned back in the carriage seat, closed her eyes, and tipped her face to absorb the last rays of sunlight.

A car backfired, or at least she thought the sound came from a car. People screamed and shouted. She opened her eyes just as Alexander shoved her to the carriage floor.

With an undignified thump, she landed on knees and elbows, her gown riding up her legs. Alexander piled on top of her, pressing her into the carpet.

"What's wrong?" she asked as the carriage driver whipped the horses into a gallop and the milling crowds turned and fled.

"Someone's shooting at us."

"At us?"

Alexander had to be wrong. Neither of them held any power. Who would want to harm them?

"Alex, is some angry husband or father after you?"

"I don't think so."

A shot pinged off the carriage, close to her head. Fear started to move up her throat and choke off her breath. This was no joke. Someone wasn't just trying to scare them.

Someone was trying to kill them.

Chapter One

Tashya knew better than to glare at her brother, Nicholas. Ever since bullets had dented the carriage, he'd been strung tight, worried over his siblings. Even during his wedding reception, while he was dancing with his bride, he had kept his siblings in sight. Now, two days later, the king should have left for the beach to enjoy his honeymoon, but he'd stayed at the palace to issue orders. Orders Tashya had no intention of obeying even if he did dispense them from behind the royal desk.

However, instead of raising her voice to match the steel in the king's, Tashya spoke softly, reasonably. "Nicholas, I'm not leaving Vashmira."

He frowned at her. "Why can't you follow Alexander to the United States? Help him open the Vashmiran embassy?"

"Because *my* work is here." Tashya had no intention of letting a few stray bullets scare her off, not when several important laws affecting women's rights would come up for a vote during the next few weeks. "Alexander jumped at the opportunity to go to Washington, D.C. He's always enjoyed traveling, but I would prefer to—"

"If you stay, you will accept my security precautions." Nicholas folded his arms over his chest.

Tashya eyed her brother warily. He didn't usually yield to her wishes quite this easily. As much as she wanted to believe his recent marriage might have lessened his stubbornness, she knew that when it came to safety issues, Nicholas could be ruthlessly intractable. Who could blame him? Last year they'd lost their father to an assassination right here within the royal office. Much more recently, the king and queen had been threatened by a bomb. Now someone had fired shots at Tashya and Alexander.

"What security precautions?" she asked.

"At my request, the Americans have sent over a special agent. His role is twofold, to protect you and to impersonate Alexander."

"That's why you kept Alex's trip so quiet and put out that fake story that he's ill." She marveled at Nicholas's ingenuity. "I thought it was merely for his safety that you didn't allow a press release. But you didn't want anyone to know he'd left Vashmira...so this agent can take his place."

"His name is Hunter Leigh." Nicholas's hand hovered over the intercom button that connected him to his secretary. "And if you stay, he's going to be constantly by your side. No arguments. I expect you to spend all your time with him. You'll help him impersonate Alexander."

The idea of spending so many hours with anyone made her shudder. She had work to do and didn't have time to coddle some American agent. "Mr. Leigh doesn't know our people, our customs or our ways. He's an outsider."

"That's why we can trust him." Nicholas keyed his secretary through the intercom.

Tashya realized that Nicholas was right. Her brother suspected someone inside the palace meant to do the royal family harm. So, naturally, he'd trust an outsider instead of the people who'd had access to the palace for years.

A voice came through the speaker phone. "Yes, Your Highness?"

"Please send in Mr. Leigh."

As soon as Hunter Leigh entered the room Tashya took one look at him and shook her head in exasperation. Hunter had brown hair; Alexander's was black. Hunter had dark eyes the color of thunderclouds, heavy brows and a commanding presence that almost crackled with vitality; blue-eyed Alex was a laid-back playboy. The contrasts didn't stop there. Hunter must have weighed a good ten kilos more than her brother, yet there wasn't an inch of fat on him. He moved like a cat, with smooth, quick, long-legged strides. Alexander had never rushed anywhere in his life—except maybe into the bed of one of his numerous lovers. If Hunter ever climbed through bedroom windows at night, she imagined he'd be on a high-stakes mission where capture would mean his death.

Tashya stared at Hunter, appreciating his masculinity and frowning at the same time. "Nicholas, there is no way this man can impersonate Alex."

"And hello to you, too, Your Highness." Hunter's words were cavalier, but he had an air of vigilance about him, the watchfulness of a man accustomed to depending on his instincts to keep him alive in dangerous situations.

"I'm sorry," she told him. Rarely did she forget

her manners. Usually people were slightly in awe of royalty, and she worked hard to put them at ease. Yet this man didn't seem impressed by their titles or the luxurious trappings of the palace. He was all business, and she sensed that he would respond best to being treated in a forthright manner. "I didn't mean to be rude, but you don't look anything like our brother."

Hunter ran a hand through his thick hair. "Give me a chance to redye my hair back to my original color before you decide. Clothes, contact lenses and body language will make a huge difference."

His confidence amused her. "Even if you were Alex's twin, you don't sound like him or move like him. And what about the language? Alexander is fluent in—"

"Russian, English, Arabic and French." Nicholas stood and shook Hunter's hand. "My sources told me you can handle the job."

"Yes, Your Majesty."

Nicholas sized the man up and clapped him on the shoulder. "Let's dispense with the titles, shall we? Alexander calls me Nicholas."

"Just what kind of work do you usually do?" Tashya asked, not the least bit sure he could pull off the impersonation. The man didn't even smell like her brother, who favored spicy and expensive colognes. His scent was more elemental, a combination of sunshine, earth and soap.

"That information's classified." Hunter looked her straight in the eye with an expression that made her think of sex in the rain—not that she'd ever had sex in the rain. He just had this down-to-earth quality combined with confidence that she found undeniably attractive. And all wrong. This man was nothing like her brother.

''And actually,'' Hunter continued, ''we don't have time for chitchat. I need you to gather videos and pictures of your brother for me. You'll have to teach me to mimic his voice and habits and movements.''

''I'm no acting instructor.''

''I need to have his intonations and movements down cold in less than a day.''

''A day?'' Tashya's jaw dropped, and she forcibly snapped her mouth closed. Didn't the best actors study their roles for months?

Hunter crossed his arms over his chest and cocked his head at an arrogant angle that Alexander never would use. ''That should just barely leave me enough time to memorize the faces and names of our guests for the upcoming ball to honor your queen. And you'll have to fill me on your brother's past relationships.''

''I did as you asked,'' Nicholas told Hunter. ''No one except me has visited Alexander since his illness. No maids. Not even his personal servants.''

''Good. Your brother's *illness* will be over in a few days.''

Tashya looked from Nicholas to Hunter and back at her brother, beginning to comprehend the much too enormous task ahead. During the last few years Alexander could have dallied with half the women at court, but he had been discreet. He rarely spoke of his conquests, so just how the hell was she supposed to brief Hunter? Nicholas had saddled her with an impossible task, but she didn't want to say so for fear her brother might return to his original idea of insisting she leave the country.

She eyed Nicholas with exasperation. "You expect him to be ready for the ball this Friday?"

"His boss assured me Hunter accomplishes the impossible on a regular basis."

"The mission is doable, but my success will depend on the princess." Hunter's voice sounded as casual as if he were discussing taking a walk-on part on the stage—not impersonating a crown Prince of Vashmira so well that not even his intimate acquaintances would be able to discern the deception.

She bristled at his implication, but kept her tone mild. "Just how will it be *my* fault—if *you* fail?"

"Because I am the best in the world at what I do."

"And modest, too?" she teased, captivated by his confidence, worried that no one could pull off the deception, at the same time realizing there was nothing simple about Hunter Leigh.

Nicholas's expression didn't change. "I've been assured through channels that Hunter has the adaptability of a chameleon and could easily have been one of Hollywood's greatest actors." Nicholas offered his hand to Hunter, nodded at Tashya. "Now, if you'll both excuse me, I promised my bride a ride through the palace grounds."

Nicholas strode from his office and left them alone. Tashya's stomach fluttered. Watching Hunter try and fail to transform himself into her brother would have been interesting and fun—except that the price for failure was too high.

"WHAT DO WE DO first?" Tashya asked Hunter with a business-like resolve he hadn't expected from a princess. She might look as if she'd stepped out of some fairy tale with her long, straight dark hair, quiet eyes and aristocratic cheekbones, but beneath the appearance of pampered princess he sensed her strength. A strength he suspected she might need to survive the coming weeks.

She might hide behind a soft and docile demeanor, but when she'd disagreed with Hunter, for just a moment, anger had flickered in her expressive eyes. Her brother, either accustomed to her acquiescence or distracted by his newly wedded state, hadn't seemed to notice that Hunter had needled a nerve or two. But Hunter felt comforted that he could penetrate her cool exterior—not very far—just enough to remind him that, although she was royalty, she was also human.

Enough about the princess, he had work to do, important work. If he completed this assignment satisfactorily, he could expect to be assigned to project Cobra next, an ultrasecret highly classified CIA assignment he'd wanted in on for the past six months. One job at a time, he reminded himself. To get started he needed his tools that, if Nicholas had filled his request, were now inside Alexander's suite. Too bad Nicholas had sealed the secret tunnels. "You must sneak me into Alexander's quarters."

"Now?" She stood and smoothed her skirt.

"It's critical to the mission's success that everyone remain under the impression Alexander is ill. Friday, when I take his place, I want people to notice the dark shadows under my eyes, not the fact that my feet are one size smaller than your brother's."

"I can slip you into his suite from my quarters," Tashya offered.

"How often do you bring a man to your rooms, Princess?"

Her eyes frosted, obviously not understanding the

connection between her statement and his question. "Nicholas may have ordered me to help you, but I have no intention of—"

"Princess, I don't give a damn about your intentions. Nor do I care if you've bedded every man in Vashmira between the ages of eighteen and eighty."

She raised an aristocratic eyebrow, a gesture she must have practiced to put men in their place without having to utter one word. Hell, he didn't have time to be delicate. Didn't have time to tiptoe around her sensibilities—not if he intended to impersonate her brother by Friday.

Still, he couldn't order her around like a lackey. He settled for making an explanation, something he rarely bothered to do. "My concern isn't personal curiosity. Will I be noticed when I enter your private suite? Will my accompanying you there cause comments?"

She pulled herself up so straight that she could have been a boot-camp recruit. "My suite of rooms includes an office, which houses two secretaries and three assistants. Dozens of people go in and out every day."

He drilled her with a stare. "And if Hunter Leigh and the princess of Vashmira stroll past all these secretaries and assistants into your office, and we don't come out for three days, will that cause talk?"

"It might." A slight blush rose up her necks to her cheeks. Clearly she didn't like answering his question and just as clearly she understood the necessity for doing so. He had to give her credit. She'd looked him straight in the eyes, then had responded without hesitation, her voice direct and calm. For some perverse reason, he wanted to pierce her shell again, but he restrained the uncharacteristic impulse.

Stick to the job. "What time does your staff leave?"

"Five o'clock."

"All right, then. I haven't slept in forty-eight hours. I'll take a nap." He sank into a chair and closed his eyes, grateful for the opportunity to rest. Long ago during his stint in the military, he'd learned to fall asleep almost immediately in what SEALs referred to as a combat nap. The ability to set his internal clock and awaken completely refreshed often came in handy. Rested minds made fewer mistakes. And he couldn't afford even one.

Hunter might regret having been pulled off an international hunt for the disgraced Peruvian spy master, Jesus Montesinos, but he was a professional. He would turn his full attention to his new assignment. He would shed his last persona as easily as a bird of prey molts its feathers. Hunter would emerge from the nest in a few days with new plumage, ready to spread his wings.

TASHYA COULDN'T BELIEVE the audacity of the newly arrived American. One moment Hunter made unthinkable demands, the next he dismissed her and fell into a deep sleep. Did he think she had nothing better to do than to baby-sit him? She almost chuckled at the thought. The man before her was certainly no baby. He was demanding, arrogant and presumptuous, and she couldn't decide whether to be amused, insulted or annoyed.

After all, she was the princess of Vashmira. Men

usually fawned over her. They were always polite. Respectful.

Hunter treated her as a partner, almost as part of a team. He had been incredibly demanding. But when his eyes had flared with approval after she'd straightforwardly answered his questions, she'd felt as if he'd given her a sincere compliment. While she was accustomed to compliments, she rarely received any that were sincere.

She'd met few men as brash or as take-charge as Hunter Leigh. While she admired him and was sure he did his job with ruthless efficiency, she didn't know if she liked him. His intensity frightened her a little, intrigued her even more.

During the time they'd spoken, he hadn't mentioned one personal thing about himself—except how long it had been since he'd last slept and that his hair wasn't naturally brown. Even in sleep, he seemed mysterious, sleeping upright in the leather chair, his head propped backward, his lips slightly parted.

She had the feeling the slightest sound would wake him—that if she touched him, he might threaten her with bodily harm before he came fully awake. Yet, she had no fear he would deliberately harm her physically. He had too much honor. No, what frightened her was something elemental that she couldn't quite name.

She would have given up her royal pearls to see his file but knew that a man of his background might not even have a file, and if he did, it probably would be fictitious. The Americans had obviously sent one of their best men, a man comfortable working alone, a man used to infiltrating the enemy. His cover story would be deep and make it difficult, if not impossible, to discover the truth.

She gazed down at the man sent to protect her. How many foes had those hands fought? His relaxed fingers rested loosely on his muscular thighs, his thick forearms, dusted with swirls of hair, were tanned and strong. A scar ran along his arm from wrist to elbow. A scar that would give him away as an imposter in a heartbeat.

Leaning closer, she eyed the scar a little more carefully, and her eyes widened with the realization that the jagged puckering of skin was due to cleverly applied makeup. He'd already admitted that his hair color wasn't his own, and she wondered how much more of his normal appearance he'd altered, and if he could possibly pull off looking like Alexander's clone.

He claimed he needed her help, but even asleep, he appeared self-sufficient, as if he trusted no one. She had to be a fool for standing over a sleeping stranger. If he was going to take up the majority of her time between now and Friday, she had to speak with her secretary and make arrangements. She had people to call and meetings to reschedule.

Throughout the afternoon, Tashya worked in her office, postponing, until after the weekend, her appointments with cabinet officials whose votes she intended to try to influence. Although she didn't expect to push through her entire agenda, Tashya wanted laws enacted to ensure women earned equal pay for equal work. She wanted much more, of course, but this issue was a priority and could not wait another year.

She tried to call Alex in the States, but he didn't

answer his phone, and she couldn't help worrying over his safety. Since their mother had died when they were children, Tashya had been extremely close to both of her brothers. Now that Nicholas was happy with his new wife, she tended to fret more over Alex.

As the clock struck five, Tashya returned to the royal office where she'd instructed Nicholas's secretary not to disturb Hunter's sleep. She found the American agent opening his eyes. "I've taken care of the items you requested. Videotapes and photographs of my brother are waiting."

"Thanks. Any word on tracking down the shooters?"

She shook her head. "We aren't hopeful. There were thousands of people lining the streets, making a getaway relatively easy. The police have yet to find any witnesses. However, they have recovered the empty cartridges—if we find the weapon, forensics can make a positive match."

"Please, keep me posted."

So, the man did have some manners. "I've also asked the kitchen to prepare some food, so we won't be disturbed for the evening."

The moment she spoke those words she realized their provocative quality, but Hunter didn't deliberately misunderstand and make some suggestive remark. He stood, stretched like a cat awakening from a satisfying sleep. Arms over his head, he bent side to side, his powerful torso flexing. Placing his hands on his trim waist, he rolled his hips in a circle, then dropped his head first to his right shoulder then the other, his bones making a noise like knuckles cracking.

At the sound she winced slightly. "Next time you

want to nap, you might pick a more comfortable spot.'' She resisted telling him they had beds in Vash-mira.

''There won't be a next time,'' Hunter murmured.

''Why not?'' He'd fallen asleep so easily she'd have thought it a regular habit.

''Does Alexander take naps?''

Point made, he fell into step beside her. Together they exited the royal office and ambled down a long corridor with mosaic tiles and Turkish carpets. Art on loan from the National Museum hung on the walls. From the crystal chandeliers to the people who politely stepped out of their path, Hunter took it all in.

She expected a million questions. Instead he matter-of-factly told her his requirements. ''I'll need a blueprint of the palace and the grounds. Maps of the country, detailed ones of the cities where Alexander has spent a lot of his time. Does he have an address book?''

She thought of his little back book with the names of people on five continents, ninety percent of them women. ''He probably took that with him.''

''There isn't a duplicate?''

The corridor widened and became busier. She chose a quieter hallway that led to her suite. Hunter's step never faltered, but his gaze moved back and forth with the vigilance of a man whose life might depend on finding his way through these corridors in the dark.

''My brother is something of a playboy, not inclined to make backups of his paperwork. He's rich, charming and titled. Women fling themselves at him with abandon.''

''If there's some woman he's particularly friendly with at the moment, Nicholas will have to find an excuse to keep her away. I'm good—but not good enough to fool someone who knows Alexander intimately.''

So, he did have some reservations. Perhaps she could save them both a lot of time and effort if she explained exactly what he was up against. ''At the ball, you'll meet many, many women who know my brother quite well.''

''They'll see what they want to see—Alexander. Changing my looks will be the easiest part of the deception.''

She didn't question him until they were safely ensconced in her offices where he again noted details with a more than observant eye. She guided him through her reception area and office then through a secluded hallway to her private rooms. Connecting her office to her living quarters had proved convenient—as had the private walk-through that connected her suite with Alexander's.

She halted and pressed the security panel, inputting the code she and Alexander shared. Hunter scrutinized her every move, no doubt committing the sequence to memory.

''Why's the lock between private apartments necessary?'' Hunter asked.

''After our troubles this past year, Ira Hanuck, our palace security chief, insisted on monitoring access by the servants and cleaning crews.''

She stepped inside Alexander's apartment, which was decorated in creams, golds and black. The rooms Alexander had claimed for his own gave evidence of his personal flair for the rich and exotic. Pictures from an African photograph safari dotted one wall. Blooming orchids hung in buckets under a huge gold-framed mirror. A gun collection rested inside locked cabinets.

Seeing Hunter's reflection reminded her once again of how different he looked from Alexander. "What did you mean when you said changing your looks is the easiest part of the deception?"

"People aren't usually as observant as you'd think. Harrison Ford is one of the most recognizable actors in the world. Put him in sunglasses and a hat on a street corner, and most people won't recognize him, but play his voice on the radio, and he'll be easily recognized."

Hunter opened Alexander's foyer closet and fingered the numerous jackets of varying colors and materials. His sharp gaze swept over the custom-leather boots lined up neatly along the floor, and then he shut the door. "Your brother's a clotheshorse?"

"Wait till you see the walk-in room off his bedroom. Every item he wears is custom tailored. Nicholas claims he'll have to raise taxes next year just to keep our brother in Armani and Versace."

She wondered if he thought Alex terribly vain, but he voiced no opinion. She waited as he thoroughly inspected every knickknack in the foyer before speaking. "That recognition factor you spoke of was a movie star's face seen by strangers. Many of the people you will meet have known my brother for years."

"Have a little faith."

She released a sigh of frustration and decided to be blunt. "I don't think you understand what you're up against."

"And you do?"

"I live here."

"And?"

"I know my brother."

"And?"

"Are you prepared to sleep with every woman who flirts with you?"

Chapter Two

"Let's just say I'm a smooth operator and leave it at that, Princess." Hunter understood why Tashya was intent on quizzing him about how he planned to impersonate her brother, but he didn't feel inclined to answer her. He had no intention of making love to any woman in Vashmira, since an amorous distraction was a surefire way to get a man killed.

Tashya didn't bother even to look over her shoulder to speak to him as she led him through Alexander's plush bachelor quarters. Luckily, Hunter had mastered multitasking. While his memory retention was not quite photographic, he could memorize and catalog the contents of each room and learn the layout while studying her stiff back and assessing her mood.

"Don't call me *princess.*" The annoyance in her tone let him know that he'd struck a sensitive nerve.

"Why not?"

"Alexander never does."

Her curt comment, meant to put him in his place, only confirmed his assessment that Tashya possessed a keen mind. Under other circumstances, he might not have been surprised. But from the extensive research he'd done on her during his flight, he knew she'd grown up pampered. He also knew she spent a good part of her free time with a stable full of Thoroughbred horses. She rode them over fences, nursed them and cared for them, not exactly a hobby for the faint of heart. She revealed a toughness by trying to influence political changes within her country. Hunter knew all too well that politics could often be a dirty business, and in this part of the world, making changes had to be even more difficult for a woman to accomplish. But again, Tashya had undertaken a task that took brains and guts and that contrasted with the debutante image she projected so well.

To her credit, although she clearly didn't like him calling her *princess,* she wouldn't say so. Instead she'd found the key to stopping him by mentioning his mission.

"What *does* Alexander call you?" he asked, hoping it wasn't *sis.*

Because no way could he think of Tashya Zared as his sister. Hunter had four sisters who'd grown up in various attractive shapes and different sizes. His mouth never went dry when he looked at their legs. In fact, he rarely noticed their figures unless they specifically asked him to approve one of their latest outfits. However, he noticed Tashya's attributes; his afternoon combat nap had been invaded by images of luminous skin, perceptive blue eyes and long, sexy legs.

She halted in the plush living area. Deep, leather, U-shaped sofas faced a wall-size television screen. Colorful, silk throw pillows embroidered with gold threads and matching tassels decorated the contemporary furniture and picked up the colors from matching lounge chairs and coordinating wallpaper. The airy room possessed high ceilings, graceful interior arches and floor-to-ceiling windows that overlooked a private courtyard with luxuriant vegetation.

"He calls me Tashya. I call him Alex or Alexander." She gestured behind a silk screen. "Your luggage is over there with the items you requested." She peered curiously at his belongings.

"What?"

"Those bags don't look as if they contain clothes."

"They don't. I'll wear Alexander's stuff." He didn't elaborate on the rest of his equipment, and although clearly curious, she didn't pry.

She turned from the luggage to face him, her features composed, her eyes direct. "I appreciate your willingness to attempt to turn yourself into Alexander, and, despite my earlier skepticism, I'll do everything I can to help you. So, what's first?"

Wow. Talk about diplomacy. She sure knew how to diffuse the tension caused by her earlier comments. However she could do nothing to ease the interest flaring in the pit of his stomach.

Keep your mind on work.

"Your help will be invaluable."

She must have heard the challenge in his tone because her brows knit downward into a slight frown. "How? Because I know Alexander?"

"Exactly. You know his looks, his speech patterns, his day-to-day habits. Can you find me a picture of your brother? The bigger the portrait and the fewer clothes he's wearing, the better."

She searched his face, her eyes round and solemn as if contemplating whether or not he was serious. Finally she nodded at some thought she didn't share, snapped her fingers and hurried toward a closed door.

"I think I know just the picture." She opened the door, stepped into a bedroom, plucked a framed picture off the wall and returned, carefully closing the door behind her. "The court photographer took this at the beach last summer."

He accepted the frame, and their fingers touched. Soft skin with delicate calluses stroked him for the briefest second, calluses from gripping the reins of one of her horses. In that fleeting moment an awareness between them stirred, kindled, flared. She must have noticed the heat, too, because she released the frame so quickly that he juggled the picture before retaining a firm grasp. Was she sensitive about being touched? Or sensitive about *his* touch?

He didn't know. Couldn't afford the distraction. Hunter's father, a Vietnam veteran, had taught him about his duty to his country before his ABCs. Hunter's job to protect this woman had to be his first priority. He couldn't afford the jolts of stimulation zinging through him, jolts that would distract him from concentrating fully on the task ahead of him.

Hunter forced his consideration from the princess to the prince's photograph. A smiling Alexander wearing a swimsuit mugged for the camera as he played volleyball on a beach. In the background, a blue sea stretched to the horizon.

"This is perfect." Walking over to his bags, Hunter hefted a bulging case, returned to Tashya and grinned at her. "My cosmetics bag. I never travel without it."

"How…charming."

He unzipped the bag and pulled out several boxes of hair color in different shades from dark brunette to black. He choose one and tossed it to her. "What do you think?"

She caught the box, peered at the advertisement and frowned. "I can't tell much from this photograph, but Alexander's hair is almost exactly the same color as mine and Nicholas's."

Again he dug into his bag and removed a pair of scissors. "A lock of Alexander's hair would be better," he noted. "But if I can't have his, how about the next best thing? Mind if I cut a lock of your hair, so I can match the color?"

"I most definitely would mind." Tashya retreated a step and folded her arms across her chest, giving him what he thought of as her haughty-imperious-princess stare.

This was the first time she'd exhibited pride in her looks, and he had to swallow a smile as he considered her very female yet restrained reaction. If he'd have made the same request to his youngest sister, she'd have laughed in his face. Sister number one, Kathy, would have slapped him upside the head, and he shuddered at what the twins, Alessa and Audrey, would have done.

He gentled his voice. "A little snip won't show. Please, turn around and lift your hair off your neck. I'll clip just one tiny wisp from underneath. It won't show," he repeated. "And it won't hurt. I promise."

She released a loud, aggravated breath, spun around and lifted her hair. Her long, graceful neck reminded him of the dancers in a show that his sisters had dragged him to. He'd expected to hate the ballet—instead he'd been mesmerized by the graceful ballerinas and, afterward, had endured his sisters's teasing for weeks.

He set the frame down on a table, then approached her with his scissors. He trailed his fingers along the base of her scalp, enjoying the freedom to touch her. As his fingers closed on a lock, she shivered. A reaction to his brief touch? Or fear that he would do permanent damage to her beautiful hair?

He lifted the scissors, giving unnecessary instructions but needing to reassure her with his voice. "You'll never miss this tiny lock of hair. Hold still." He cut the piece in one clean snip. "Perfect."

TASHYA LOWERED HER HAIR slowly, reluctant to turn around to face Hunter until she reined in her galloping emotions. How could the slightest graze of his fingertips along her neck make her feel so weak? Her experience with the Toad, the crown prince of Moldova, had turned her off men for the past few months.

While she enjoyed her position in the royal family, she hated being courted solely because of her position and title, or for political reasons.

Unfortunately, she longed for someone to want *her*—not for her wealth or her position—but for herself. So far, she'd met several men who met those requirements, men who were wealthy and powerful in their own right. However, she had felt nothing special for any of them.

Now she was reacting to Hunter, a man she barely knew and probably didn't like. She gathered that he took his assignment to impersonate her brother seriously and wasn't here to ingratiate himself with the royal family or with her. He offered little or no idle conversation to fill the uncomfortable silences. For all she knew, he didn't notice the awkwardness of their forced togetherness.

Furthermore, she doubted that she and Hunter had anything in common. They came from different countries, different ethnic backgrounds, different social strata. Yet something in her responded to him on a level she couldn't name. Fed up with herself, wondering if she would ever find the happiness that Nicholas shared with Ericka, she finally gathered her courage and turned around.

He was gone.

She hadn't heard a footstep or a whisper of air. Had no indication Hunter could move as quietly as a shadow. Apparently, without saying a word, he'd headed into the bedroom, leaving the door open, as if in silent invitation for her to follow.

Tashya didn't go into bedrooms with men she didn't know. Especially not a sinfully decadent bedroom with its princely bed and deluxe black-satin coverlet, plump cream-and-gold pillows and drapes thick enough to block all sunlight.

She heard water running in the shower. Hunter must have headed straight through the bedroom and into the bathroom to dye his hair. An image of him naked in the shower seeped into her mind, his broad shoulders and his powerful chest tapering to a flat stomach, lean hips and legs. His muscular arms belonged to the man whose arousing fingertips had grazed her neck, creating the most disturbing sensation. A sensation she neither wanted to acknowledge nor to analyze. She'd much prefer that the sensual images of him stayed out of her head, but she seemed to have no control over the path her thoughts kept taking.

She was no teenager subject to the whims of erratic and out-of-control hormones and fully believed she could make a rational decision over whom she felt an attraction to. She most definitely didn't yearn for the excitement of falling for some military, secret agent man who'd charged into her life and who would vanish when his mission was over.

Oh, no. She might not recognize exactly what she wanted, but she knew what she *didn't* want. She didn't want to think about Hunter as a romantic possibility. Didn't even want to consider him taking a shower. Didn't want to think about why she'd had such a powerful response to his touch.

When he paraded out of the bathroom with only a towel twisted around his hips, she felt as if her horse had just leapt a six-foot fence and left her two giant strides behind. Her breath hitched.

Hunter's wet black hair was slicked back from his forehead. His naked chest with its curly black hair sent her pulse into a heated canter. She had to remind herself to breathe.

Hunter paid no attention to her. He removed a cape from his bag, spread it over the floor and stood in front of a full-length mirror. With tweezers, he began to pluck his hairline and eyebrows, occasionally consulting Alexander's picture. Then, while she watched in fascination, he gave himself a quick haircut, used Alexander's custom gel and blew his hair dry. Finally, after consulting the picture, he cut his sideburns a quarter inch shorter. The change of hair color and style made a remarkable difference, but not enough.

Padding to her brother's closet, he opened the door and whistled at the huge space. Alexander probably had fifty suits in blue, another fifty or so in black and just as many in beige and white. One wall was lined with hundreds of shirts, another with dress shoes in the softest Italian leather, sneakers from lines endorsed by runners, cyclists and N.B.A. stars, fine English riding boots and sandals in every color and style imaginable.

He glanced from the clothes to her, his expression reminding her of a determined and uncomfortable lover shopping for lingerie for his sweetheart—resolute, but at a complete loss.

She barely recalled her intention to avoid the bedroom and stepped over the threshold. ''Need some help?''

''Please. What would Alexander wear on a casual evening spent in his room?''

''Normally, his manservant lays out his clothes, but he's on vacation. You need to remember that Alexander is extremely fastidious about his appearance and may reject Alan's choice.'' She plucked a dress shirt and casual slacks off their hangers, added a leather belt, shoes and socks.

''What about underclothes?''

She shrugged but didn't bother restraining a grin of amusement. ''Alexander doesn't wear any.''

Hunter winced. ''You aren't kidding, are you?''

''My brother claims underwear binds the crown jewels.''

Hunter carried the clothes back to the bathroom. ''Does he often make bad jokes?''

Apparently he didn't expect an answer because he shut the door, only to return minutes later. She looked and then looked again. He really had begun to resemble Alexander. Yet, a keen examination by anyone close to her brother would reveal Hunter's deception.

''I'm not done yet,'' he said, as if reading her thoughts.

Once again he rooted into his cosmetics bag, and this time he removed several sets of colored contact lenses. After gently placing the lenses into his eyes, sky-blue replaced his normal gray, and his resemblance to Alexander startled her. Perhaps, he really might pull off the subterfuge.

When he reached into his magic bag this time, she forgot to breathe. She didn't recognize the white objects. Opening his mouth, he placed one set of caps over his upper teeth, another set over his lowers.

"What are you doing?"

"Your brother's teeth are shaped and colored differently from mine. These caps fix the problem."

"How can you speak with those things in your mouth? Isn't that uncomfortable?"

"No more than walking around without underwear," he muttered in a deliciously husky grumble that sounded nothing like Alex.

She recalled that he'd told her changing his appearance was the easy part, and now she understood what he'd meant. If Hunter stood absolutely still and said nothing, she might for a short second believe he was her brother—but not for a moment longer. His posture was stiffer, straighter. He held his head at a different angle and even his small movements were a dead giveaway.

Hunter moved with the sleek economy of motion of a ninja fighter. Alexander's gestures tended to be grand and larger than life. Exuberant and flashy. Hunter possessed an inner stillness that radiated calm. Alexander was full of life.

"You said you had videotapes of your brother?" Hunter strode back into the living room and she followed.

"There's a stack of tapes on top of the VCR." She settled into a chair. "I hope you know how to work it. I'm not great with mechanical devices."

She didn't mention that every time she wanted to record a program she had to ask for help. Didn't understand why the VCRs had to be so complicated.

Hunter had no difficulty. He popped the tape into the machine, then fiddled with two remote controls. Alexander, wearing one of his ceremonial uniforms, appeared on the large-screen television, walking alongside Nicholas during the coronation ceremony.

"This is a recent tape?" Hunter asked. He didn't sit. Instead he watched the tape, then used the remote to rewind a segment.

By the fourth or fifth replay, Tashya had grown bored. She wanted to call Alex again, to make sure he was okay. She wanted to check with Nicholas's secretary, to remind her not to schedule him too heavily over the first few weeks of his marriage. In the early evening, she often helped her stepmother bath the baby and tuck in her half brothers, Dimitri and Nikita. She'd had a long day, and clearly Hunter didn't need her to study the tapes. About to say goodbye, she caught a movement out of the corner of her eye.

Alex? For a moment she'd thought he had returned, then she chided herself. Hunter was mimicking Alexander's walk, his posture, his demeanor. It was amazing. He had him down in less than half an hour. "That's remarkable."

"I'm trying to establish muscle memory."

"What's that?"

"Do you have a saying over here that once you learn to ride a bike, you'll never forget?"

She nodded.

"The reason you don't forget is mostly due to muscle memory. The brain is good at establishing patterns. I'm trying to brand Alexander's patterns over my own. They need to be instinctive, so that if I flirt with a pretty girl, or issue an order, or protect you, I don't return to old habits."

"How long does this branding take?"

"Usually several weeks. I'm rushing things a bit." He turned and paced in the opposite direction.

"You lost Alex's timing for an instant during that turn. My brother moves his arms more."

"Like this?" He turned again.

"You really are good at this."

She suspected that imitating her brother was not all he was good at and that Hunter would be just as good at doubling as her bodyguard as any security agent in the palace, probably better. Her confidence in Hunter soared as she watched him take on Alexander's traits, one after the other. Although she hadn't realized how tense she'd been since the shots had been fired into their carriage after the wedding, she now felt herself relaxing a little.

With Hunter at her side until palace security caught the shooter, she would be safe enough to continue her normal activities. Critical votes would soon take place in the cabinet. She planned to lobby hard to see that legislation ensuring women's rights was enacted in Vashmira. Hunter would protect her while she worked.

Suddenly a terrible thought struck her. They'd all assumed that her father's assassination last year had been solved and that Nicholas's and Ericka's problems were over. But with the recent shooting at her and Alexander, palace security was looking for a conspiracy. However, those shots might have had nothing to do with their former problems. Suppose someone wanted to stop her from her work?

Hunter reviewed another portion of the tape where Alexander sat and another where he stood. "Does he always pull up his slacks before he sits?"

"Yes."

"Okay. Now tell me what has you frowning so hard you're going to put a permanent crease in your forehead."

She saw no harm in sharing her thoughts. After all, if he was to protect her, he needed to understand palace political intrigues. "Next week, our cabinet is voting on some issues dear to my heart. Women's rights."

"And?"

"I was wondering at the possibility of someone who opposed my ideas maybe trying to silence me by shooting me."

She thought he might slough off her idea and was pleased when he took her seriously. "Are tempers running high over these issues?"

"Very high."

"Okay." He handed her a pad of paper and a pen. "Make a list of everyone who opposes your views."

She didn't bother reaching for the pen and paper. "Everyone but Nicholas and Alexander opposes my ideas. Even my stepmother, Sophia."

"Sophia is your father's widow and second wife?"

"Yes. She believes a woman's place is in the home."

"And you don't?"

"I believe a woman's place is anywhere she wishes to be."

"Even in the military?"

How easily he'd put his finger on the crux of the problem. "General Vladimir is adamant that no woman shall ever serve. He won't even speak with me about the subject, but..."

"But?"

"I have a meeting with his aide, Major Stephan Cheslav, and am hoping he'll help me to change the general's mind or to at least soften his hard-line stance."

"Who else is resisting?"

"The secretary of state, the chief economic adviser, even our press secretary."

"Are any of their personal positions threatened by the changes you'd like to make?"

"I have no idea, but that's a good question to keep in mind as I speak with them next week." She eyed him with amazement as he placed another tape into the VCR, his movements so like Alexander's she became distracted.

Between the cosmetic changes to his body, Alexander's clothes and now his careful study of movement, he really looked like her brother. Funny how she hadn't seen the similarities earlier. He and her brother shared the same proud nose, aristocratic cheekbones and facial structure. The Americans had chosen their man carefully and well.

At a knock on the door, she jumped, nervous that anyone would interrupt them. Hunter wasn't ready for company. He had yet to master Alexander's voice and speech patterns.

"If you were with your sick brother, who would

answer the door?'' Hunter asked, reaching toward his luggage.

''I would.''

''Okay. Let's go.''

From one of his bags, he removed a black semi-automatic revolver. He held the weapon as casually as she ate dinner with a fork. The thought only increased her nervousness. They walked through the apartment to the front door, her heart tripping in her chest.

Hunter flattened himself against the wall and motioned for her to open the door. She did as he suggested, wondering if the food she'd ordered earlier had finally arrived. Her stomach rumbled in hunger and she pulled open the door.

Instead of someone from the kitchen, a servant offered Tashya a bouquet of flowers. ''Highness, these might perk up the prince.''

''Thank you.'' She accepted the bouquet, shut the door, and sniffed the fragrant flowers.

Her eyes widened with alarm. ''They're ticking.''

Chapter Three

"We're out of here."

Terror froze Tashya's feet to the floor. Hunter ripped the ticking bouquet from her hands and tossed the flowers into Alexander's foyer closet. After opening the apartment door, he shoved her through, then slammed it behind them.

"Run."

Hunter grabbed Tashya and pulled her down the private corridor. Together they tore down the empty hall, Hunter talking the entire time. "When we meet up with security, you have to do all the explaining. I'll pose as Alexander, but I can't be caught speaking. Tell them I have laryngitis."

How could he so calmly plan their next move when they might soon be dead? Any second she expected to hear the roar of an explosion behind her. Her heart thudded so loudly that she felt a rushing in her ears. Her lungs burned for air, and her scalp broke into a sweat.

After they rounded the corner, Hunter slid to a stop in front of an intercom. "Inform security of the problem."

She slapped the toggle. "This is Princess Tashya. Get me the chief of security. Now."

Two seconds later Ira's steady voice responded. "Yes, Highness?"

"There's a bomb in my brother's quarters."

"The king's?"

"No, Alex's. We're both in the—"

Thunder cut off her words. Hunter flattened her against the wall, protecting her with his body. With his chest pressed against her back, his hips tight to hers, he clasped his hands on her shoulders, but she'd never felt less safe.

Hot air surged down the halls and bits of plaster rained from the ceiling. Chandeliers shook, their crystals tinkling ominously. A Monet painting crashed to the floor, setting off an alarm. Smoke billowed down the hall like grasping tentacles.

Through the heat and smoke of the storm breaking around her, Hunter cradled her protectively. "We're going to be fine. The bomb wasn't big enough to do much damage."

Not much damage? She shuddered.

"When Ira gets here, ask him to find out who delivered those flowers to the gate and which guards inspected the vase before allowing it into the palace. Also, where are the men who are supposed to be guarding your apartment? I want to know every person who had contact with those flowers."

Hunter probably issued more instructions, but when she started to shake so hard she almost bit her tongue, she couldn't concentrate on his directions. Twice this week someone had tried to kill her. While he might be accustomed to this kind of harrowing fear, she wasn't. She'd started to tremble and couldn't seem to stop. Nausea made her head reel and her stomach cramp.

Someone was trying to kill her.

The bullets fired at her had seemed unreal. She'd heard the shots, but her brother had kept her safely on the carriage floor. This time she'd held a ticking bomb in her hands. If she hadn't smelled the flowers, she might be dead.

She swallowed hard, refusing to be sick, but couldn't quell her trembling. "I'm cold."

"You're in shock."

In one swift move, Hunter swept her into his arms. Surprised, she didn't move a muscle. He'd lifted her as if she weighed no more than fluff. She should protest or throw her arms around his neck to hold on, but she concentrated on breathing. This might be the most romantic thing that had ever happened to her, but she was too damned upset to enjoy the simple pleasure of a strong man's arms around her. She just prayed she wouldn't be sick all over him.

Away from the smoke and dust, Hunter found a window seat, and gently set her on it. The setting sun shot rays of orange and gold through the window and reflected a cheerful rainbow on the walls, reminding her that although the world looked pretty and peaceful, there were hidden dangers in these palace walls.

Dizzy, she swayed. Her vision blurred.

Hunter forced her to place her head down between her knees. "You'll be okay."

"Sorry...to be...so much...trouble." She took several deep breaths. "Thank you for saving my life."

"Just doing my job."

He sounded so cold, yet his gentle hands on her

shoulders were warm and comforting. The contradictions about him made her wary, and he rattled her in a way that made her uncomfortable.

Without him, she might be dead.

She had to pull herself together. She figured she had maybe sixty seconds before security showed up. By then she had to be strong enough to talk for both of them.

"I was so scared."

"Only a fool wouldn't be afraid of a ticking bomb, and one thing you're not is a fool."

But she felt foolish. She was perfectly fine. She didn't even have a scratch, but she couldn't stop shaking. "I froze when I heard the ticking."

"Don't second-guess your instincts. You ran when you had to. You did exactly what you needed to do to save your life."

She sniffed back tears. She wasn't going to cry. At least not until she reached her own room where no one would see her break down. She might feel as weak as a newborn, but she had some pride.

Hunter had come through for her when she'd needed him. Now, she had to gather enough strength to protect his cover. Slowly she raised her head and saw Ira heading directly toward them. To a stranger the palace security chief might look fierce, but she welcomed the appearance of his craggy face and stern visage.

"Are you both all right?" Ira asked, seemingly not the least suspicious of Hunter aka Alexander. Tashya wondered, not for the first time, if Nicholas should replace their chief of security. Ira was getting old, but he'd been one of her father's closest friends and these days, they needed loyalty as much as they needed top-notch security. Ira looked her over for injuries. "Do you require the royal physician?"

"We're fine. I was just a little dizzy for a moment," she said, "and Alex still has terrible laryngitis. He can't talk, but we have no need for the doctor."

"Highness, can you tell me exactly what happened?" Ira asked, motioning several of his men toward Alex's apartment. "Don't touch anything until I arrive. Just cordon off the area," he instructed his men before turning back to her.

Tashya thought she saw Hunter's approval of Ira's orders—maybe he was still doing a decent job under difficult circumstances—then Hunter squeezed her shoulder in a brotherly fashion, encouraging her to speak. Most of her trembling had ceased, but she still felt weak and light-headed.

Ira looked at Alexander, and she licked her bottom lip and cleared her throat, calling the security chief's attention back to her. "As you know, Alex has been sick. I was visiting. A servant knocked on the door and I opened it." She deleted the part about Hunter staying out of sight with his weapon. She wondered where he'd hidden the gun but didn't dare look at him.

"Did you recognize the servant?"

"Yes, but he's new, and I don't recall his name."

"Go on."

"I accepted the flowers and sniffed them. That's when I heard the ticking inside the vase. Alex grabbed the vase, dumped the flowers in the front closet and got us out of there fast. We ran a safe distance, and then I called security and the bomb went off."

"How much time went by between your accepting the flowers and your fleeing Alex's quarters?"

"Maybe a minute? Why?"

"I want that servant found. And where were the guards posted outside Alex's door? You didn't see them when you ran out?"

"I didn't notice if the guards were there or not. I assumed the servant must have taken the hallway that leads back to the central offices."

Ira's radio beeped. He removed it from his belt, held it to his mouth. "Yes?"

"The guards are dead. And we think we found the servant who delivered the flowers, sir."

Beside her, Hunter tensed. However, he remained silent and in absolute princely character.

"I want to question the servant right away."

"I'm afraid that's impossible, sir. He's dead, too."

IRA LEFT HUNTER and Tashya alone in the corridor. Tashya's color was finally returning, but she still trembled, although she bravely tried to hide it. The princess had done a fine job of speaking when she'd had to under the most difficult of circumstances, and his respect for her rose a notch. Unfortunately he couldn't allow her to rest for long. His role needed much more study and practice before he could afford to go public as the prince. The sooner he could move back into the private areas of the palace, the better.

But he also had pressing concerns about how Ira intended to investigate the bombing. Hunter itched to see the scene of destruction, to search for clues and to do a background check on the dead man.

After looking around carefully to make sure no one

would hear his words, Hunter spoke softly to Tashya. "Are you up to walking?"

She hesitated and bit her bottom lip. "I'm not sure." However, she shoved herself to her feet with a determination that no longer took him by surprise.

"I need to see Alexander's apartment."

"Why?"

"Bombs always leave pieces behind. It's like a fingerprint or a signature—unique to their makers."

"Alex would never go back to investigate—"

"I know." Her brother probably wouldn't worry over his possessions or the mess. Possessions could easily be replaced and servants would clean up his mess. Others would repair the damage—all without the prince having to lift a finger.

"It's Ira's job to—"

"Yes. But who oversees Ira?"

"You suspect Ira might have—"

"Who would find it easier than your security chief to plant a bomb in Alex's quarters?"

"I look at you and see my brother, but Alex doesn't ever think the way you do."

"And how do I think?" he asked curiously.

"You evaluate everyone with new eyes. While we've known the security chief since we were children and implicitly trust him, you are suspicious."

"Now you understand why Nicholas insisted on bringing in an outsider." He imagined she'd find it painful to suspect old family friends, relatives and trusted servants, but he figured she needed to hear the truth.

"Until we find the bomber, we have to suspect everyone."

"Well, you also have to act like a prince, and Alexander wouldn't immerse himself in the middle of Ira's investigation.''

"Would he return to his apartment for some clothing and personal items?"

She shook her head. "He'd send a servant."

"Think. You know him well. I need a reason Alexander would go back to that room."

"If he were worried about the royal treasure..."

"What treasure?"

"There's a safe in his suite where he keeps diamond-studded cuff links, assorted emerald and ruby rings, a diamond-encrusted watch and several jeweled daggers."

"Good. Where's the safe?"

She didn't even hesitate. "Behind a picture of our father and mother in his bedroom."

"Perfect." He held out his hand to her. "Let's go."

She looked at his hand, but didn't take it. "But you don't know the safe's combination."

"True."

He said no more, unwilling to tell her about skills she might consider unsavory. His princess had had quite enough shocks for one day. He waited, hand outstretched, and finally she took it.

"Every time an attempt has been made on my life, I've been with Alexander." She walked beside him, dropped his hand and linked her arm through the crook of his elbow.

The corridor remained empty. Hunter supposed Ira had men blocking off the area while he conducted his investigation. The privacy allowed them to speak without being overheard, but even so, he kept his voice low. "It could be a coincidence that you happened to be with your brother. Or maybe someone wants both of you dead.''

She frowned. ''For a while I thought that perhaps someone wanted to stop me from my work—but Alex has nothing to do with it. And the flowers weren't sent to me, but to Alex...''

''Yes. But whoever sent them may have guessed you would answer his door. We cannot rule out the possibility that someone wants to stop you.''

She pulled herself up straighter and her voice strengthened with resolve. ''These issues are important to me. I won't give up.''

''You may have no choice,'' he cautioned her mildly.

''There's always a choice. I won't be cowed by—''

They approached a side corridor, and she glanced down the hall to find Ira standing over the dead body of a servant. Between two gloved fingers, he held a tiny object up to the light, then slipped it into a plastic bag. When he saw them approach, he casually pocketed the bag.

While the gesture could have been completely innocent, Hunter's instincts kicked in. Was the security chief simply doing his job? Or was he hiding evidence?

''Find anything?'' Tashya asked, doing her best to look anywhere but directly at the body.

''I don't think the explosion killed him,'' Ira told them. ''I won't be sure until after the autopsy, but he has one hell of a bruise on the back of his head.''

''Couldn't he have been struck by flying debris?'' Tashya asked, and Hunter realized she was feigning interest for his sake—and doing a damn fine job of asking the right questions.

Ira nodded. "That's what we thought." He spread out his hands. "But we found no object that could do that kind of damage beside the body."

"Could he have been struck and then staggered here?"

"I'm afraid not. From the angle of his neck, I believe it's broken."

The servant could have been part of a conspiracy and killed by a cohort, but Hunter suspected the servant *was* an innocent. After he'd unknowingly done his dirty deed and delivered the bomb, he'd been murdered so he couldn't be questioned. Probably by the same person who'd planted the bomb in the flowers.

Right now, all they had were dead ends.

THE FULL FORCE of the bomb had blasted out from the foyer closet and toward the central palace corridors. As a result, beyond the demolished front entrance, Alexander's quarters had suffered relatively minor damage.

The security chief had informed Nicholas of the security breach, and Tashya had begged her brother not to rush over. He needed to spend time with his new bride, and there was nothing he could do here.

Hunter and Tashya skirted the blackened mosaic tiles, giving him the opportunity to casually observe the security chief's team in action. He couldn't fault the work in progress. The forensics team methodically collected the bomb's tiniest pieces with tweezers, then labeled and stored them. One member photographed the damage from every angle while another recorded the scene on videotape.

After they passed the team and moved deeper into Alex's suite, the destruction seemed minimal. A few pictures hung on the walls at odd angles, magazines had blown across the floor and one lamp had fallen.

A quick check of the exterior of Hunter's "luggage" showed no damage. Pleased that his mission hadn't been compromised, Hunter's attention returned to Tashya.

She ambled through the rooms, her head held high, looking every inch a royal, but he knew the pretense cost her. He doubted she'd even stopped trembling; however, all but the keenest of observers would never know it.

Even though none of the security team appeared to have gone this deep into the suite, he didn't dare speak. Next thing on his agenda had to be mastering Alex's voice, modulation and accent.

Tashya headed straight for the bedroom and the safe. Hunter realized her worry about giving him a reason to return had been for naught. No one questioned the prince and princess. Yet, experience told him it was always better to have a story prepared.

Tashya stopped shy of the bedroom door. Hunter had noticed her hesitancy to join him there earlier, no doubt for propriety's sake. But even if he were so inclined, he would hardly make a move on her with palace security freely wandering around.

"I thought I heard a woman's voice."

In Alex's bedroom? He placed a hand inside his pocket where he'd hidden his gun. With his free hand he jerked his thumb at the door.

Tashya nodded and waited to let him make the decision here. He leaned close and whispered, "Could be more palace security."

"There are no females in palace security."

He hoped one of Alex's paramours hadn't sneaked into the bedroom. Lovers noticed details that other people didn't.

He considered backing away and sending in security, but he needed to act as Alex would, and from what Tashya had told him, the prince would probably welcome a visitor, although maybe not even he would pull out the Welcome mat under these circumstances. If he entered the bedroom, he'd have preferred to do so with his weapon drawn—but again, Alex would never do so.

So Hunter settled for keeping his hand in his pocket. Motioning Tashya back, he opened the door. A slender woman with pale skin and worried brown eyes stood next to a man wearing a uniform that indicated he was in the Vashmiran military.

"Sophia, what are you and Stephan doing here?" Tashya asked.

Hunter already knew that Sophia was Tashya's stepmother. Now a widow, she lived in the palace with her three sons—sons who would inherit the throne if anything happened to Nicholas, Alexander and Tashya, which put her at the top of his list of suspects. She had motive, plus she had free access to the palace and plenty of opportunity to sneak bombs into flower vases.

Tashya had been smart to identify the strangers in an innocent way. Hunter had also picked up from the way she said the man's name that she didn't like him. In another lifetime, she might have made a terrific operative.

"Have you seen Dimitri and Nikita?" Sophia asked, her tone worried.

Dimitri and Nikita were her sons and at five and three years old, too young to be considered suspects.

Tashya sighed. "Are they roaming again?"

"I'm afraid so. With their propensity for turning up wherever trouble arises, I came here first. Thank goodness they aren't here."

Tashya sighed. "I think we need to assign the boys guards who know more about children." The princess's eyes turned to Stephan.

"The major insisted on accompanying me."

"Madame shouldn't be alone at a time like this," the major said.

Major Stephan Cheslav had curly chestnut hair, a neat mustache one shade lighter and skin so pale Hunter wondered if he ever went outside. He spoke with a Slavic accent, and the gleam in his eyes revealed his interest in Sophia. If Hunter were to believe the byplay, they didn't know one another well—however he never assumed the obvious to be true.

Stephan smiled at Sophia. "I feared the bomb's damage might be worse than it was. It could have been dangerous—"

"You were correct to accompany her," Tashya told him, albeit reluctantly. "What I don't understand is how the boys could have sneaked in here past the guards. All the secret tunnels have been closed."

Sophia spoke softly. "They like to hide in the laundry carts. And they are especially good at climbing under the furniture and behind the draperies."

Hunter was aware that the children had recently discovered secret passageways in the palace, but King Nicholas had ordered them sealed. Hunter, too, wanted to know if Sophia really thought the children could have entered Alex's private apartment. Was she simply using that as an excuse to be here since she'd been caught where she had no right to be?

"I think Dimitri knows the entrance code to the apartment," Sophia said. "I'm sorry, Alex. Perhaps you should have Ira change them again, but I know how much you hate memorizing the new ones."

Hunter nodded and touched his throat. He mouthed, *It's okay,* but didn't speak the words.

Neither Sophia nor Stephan seemed the least bit suspicious about his identity. Good.

A few minutes later Sophia and Stephan exited the room, Sophia telling him to rest and get well soon and promising to let them know when she found the boys. Tashya closed the door behind them.

"That was odd," Hunter said softly.

"What?"

"Finding Sophia and Stephan in this room."

Tashya almost grinned. Her natural healthy color was back, making her eyes sparkle. "You won't think Sophia's behavior's so odd after you meet my little brothers."

"Yeah, but I find it hard to believe Dimitri knows the security code. He's only five, right?"

"Five years old and going on twenty." She shrugged. "Alexander may have given him the code. Or he may have simply been careless and let Dimitri watch him enter it one too many times."

"But Sophia just walked right into the suite without even asking permission."

"She knows Alex wouldn't mind. And she had to be terrified that at the same time a bomb went off the boys are missing. I don't find her behavior all that strange. However, Major Stephan Cheslav is another matter."

"Why don't you like him?"

Tashya shrugged. "It's nothing I can put my finger on. He's a little too ambitious for my taste."

"Do Sophia and Stephan know one another well?"

"I doubt it. She probably just bumped into him on her search, and he escorted her here out of fear for her safety."

"Maybe. But why was the bedroom door shut?" Hunter asked.

This time, she paused, eyeing him with something very akin to aggravation. "Dimitri and Nikita might hide under a bed…or behind a door."

Before he said another word, the intercom beeped. Tashya walked over and flipped the switch. "Yes?"

"Nicholas has Dimitri and Nikita in the stable," Ira's voice came in clearly over the speaker. "Apparently there was a simple mixup in communications between their nanny and their mother. Sophia said you wanted to know they were okay."

"Thanks."

"Oh, one more thing. Our deceased flower deliverer's name was Hans Schultz. He's from Sophia's hometown."

Chapter Four

Three days later palace carpenters had repaired the prince's foyer, and Hunter had proclaimed his readiness to impersonate Alexander in public. Dressed in her brother's charcoal uniform, which had required only minor alterations, he looked every inch the royal prince. Although Tashya had been with Hunter almost every step of the way during his transformation, she still found the results remarkable.

After hour upon hour of practice, Hunter could modulate his voice to match her brother's, mimic his accent and had even committed to memory Alexander's pet phrases. When his voice was tired from talking, he'd memorized from pictures the faces and names of the palace staff, Nicholas's cabinet and Alex's former lady friends. However, there was no way Tashya could inform Hunter about her brother's intimate memories and attitudes concerning every person he knew.

Tashya couldn't tell him what she didn't know about Alex's private life. Hunter didn't seem concerned over these unavoidable gaps; yet, one wrong statement of agreement or denial would give away the ruse. Her stomach fluttered like a foal's on its first walk out of the birthing stall. She didn't know whether or not to be pleased by Hunter's stupendous progress or to damn his incredible confidence for believing he could pull this off. But if he failed, it wouldn't be due to lack of hard work and diligence. Hunter had the capacity to work almost 'round the clock. While he claimed he didn't have a photographic memory, he never seemed to forget anything, from the name of his valet's dog to Alex's favorite rum raisin ice cream. Now they were about to test him, and she'd probably forgotten to mention hundreds of relevant details.

After so many relentless hours of coaching him, her body had demanded sleep, but Hunter had stayed awake studying the palace blueprints and Vashmira's geography, including its cities and streets. He'd gone through Alex's credit card statements and the palace guest registry to learn about visiting merchants and the stores where the prince's purchases had been made. He studied the phone records and absorbed each telephone number and to whom it belonged. But what had they missed?

She felt like twisting her hands but forced her fingers to remain still. Revealing her own nerves would only hamper his efforts. Besides, long ago she'd learned that if she wanted to be treated with respect, and not as some spoiled princess, she mustn't reveal any weakness. As Zared's only female child, she'd often pretended to an outward calm, acting as strong as her brothers. Even if she quaked inside, she would maintain her poise.

Tashya reached up to straighten Hunter's collar, a service she'd often performed for her brother. But with Alex, the gesture had never seemed so intimate, and after smoothing flat the edges, she stepped back quickly.

"Hunter, if you don't feel ready for the ball, we could claim that Alex is still sick."

"I'm ready and so are you."

He patted her shoulder just like Alexander did, smiled at her with just the right amount of teeth showing, stared at her out of eyes the exact same blue as her brother's, and with Alex's spicy cologne, he even smelled like him. So why was she so aware of Hunter Leigh? Why couldn't she keep her feelings toward him sisterly?

Just because he looked handsome as sin, just because his eyes seemed to cling to hers a bit longer than necessary, just because her pulse leapt for no apparent reason did not mean that anything special was between them.

She sighed. Maybe if she kept lying to herself she might believe it. For the past few days they'd eaten every meal together, spent hour after hour conversing about Vashmira's economy, history and culture. They'd discussed Alex's mannerisms, from how he flirted with women to the way he chewed broccoli.

No one could keep up their guard under such circumstances. His constant proximity had taken a toll on her normal barriers. In a short time, Hunter had gained her utmost respect. Now she was worried that he would succeed in this mission and set himself up as a target.

Although she'd lived most of her life with the knowledge that the assassination of royalty was always a possibility, he had no idea what it was like always to be on guard, always be wary of strangers. When she was a child, her parents had depended on palace security to dog her footsteps to and from the backyard sandbox. By the time of her first date, she'd learned to live with the fact that she could be targeted by terrorists or political extremists. However, she had never chosen to be a target. Hunter had voluntarily accepted this mission.

Before meeting him, she would have thought that anyone who so willingly risked his life would be cold and filled with macho bravado. Yet Hunter never behaved as though he thought of himself as James Bond. He didn't rely on gadgets or physical strength as much as he depended on his best weapon—his intelligence. He prepared as if success might hinge on the tiniest detail. And he was warm—not just to the touch, but inside where it counted.

One night she'd fallen asleep on the sofa, and she'd wakened to discover that he'd tucked a blanket around her. After that, he made sure she got more rest. He'd never once made one move in her direction, and she found that she almost wanted him to.

Almost. There was no point in allowing herself to become involved with a man with a career like Hunter's. He'd be here for a week or two and then be sent back to South America or the Far East or wherever his job took him next. Her practical side told her that any deep involvement with Hunter could only hurt her, since there was no possible future for them. Yet, her sensual side wanted…she didn't know what she wanted.

Now, about to accompany him to the ball, she had to remember to treat him like a brother. With him looking so much like Alex, it shouldn't be difficult. She was determined that, if his impersonation failed, it would not be due to any slipup on her part.

When he slid a lethal-looking derringer into his coat pocket and checked the mirror for bulges, she bit back a protest. Although Alex would never carry a weapon, Hunter had the right to defend himself.

"How do I look?" he asked her, and she knew he wasn't fishing for a compliment but requesting confirmation that he'd mimicked Alexander in every possible detail.

"You're perfect." She gestured to his pocket and the gun. "But you'll set off the metal detectors."

He flipped open a large velvet box and removed a heavy gold chain that had been in the family when they were still members of the Russian nobility. "Nicholas has already thought of that. He says this little ornament sets off the metal detectors every time and that the palace guards won't even give the alarm a second thought, never mind search me."

"If they did search you, what else would they find?" she asked curiously.

"The usual."

She arched an eyebrow, testing him, wondering if he'd mention the dagger he'd shoved up his sleeve. "The usual?"

"Three guns. One in my pocket, one holstered under my arm, a third strapped to my ankle. Then there's the knife up my sleeve, a garrote, two—" He must have seen that his words disturbed her. "And my cereal box decoder ring," he teased.

"How can you joke about—"

"Protecting your life, Princess?" He reminded her of the reason he was here.

"I told you not to call me that."

"We aren't in public yet," he argued. Then he

turned and gallantly offered her his arm. "Have I told you how lovely you look this evening?"

She wasn't about to let him charm her out of her nerves. She could suppress them herself when necessary, when in public. "Have you also noticed how many doubts I have that you can pull this off?"

"Relax." He picked up her hand, placed it on his arm and winked at her. "I told you, I'm good at deception. Wait until you see me in action."

"But we can't have anticipated every contingency. Suppose we meet someone who knows Alex, and we don't know who he or she might be? We've gone over the guest list but visitors are allowed to bring a date. Or suppose you don't recognize someone from their picture? Suppose someone asks you a question, and you respond differently than Alex would?"

Hunter laughed and urged her from the suite. "That's what makes my job so much fun."

"YOU THINK YOUR job is fun?" Tashya's eyes brimmed with merriment, perhaps a little forced, but she had an inner strength that she could call on to cope with her doubts. Hunter was glad she'd banished the shadows he'd seen there earlier. She was worrying entirely too much. Trying to hide her feelings probably only added to her unease.

She squeezed his arm lightly. "Your life is never going to seem as pleasurable after you've become accustomed to being a prince."

"Just don't forget who I am," he warned softly, right before he swept her out the door of Alex's suite.

Two palace guards fell into step behind them. He thought the security might cause her to tense, but then realized that she expected them to be around her.

So far, he'd tried to immerse himself deeply enough into the role of her brother to react to her as if she were really his sister. Unfortunately she'd worn some stunning red number that hugged her curves and made his mouth water. Hunter didn't allow himself to think about women while he was on a mission. He wasn't a monk, usually relaxing between assignments with career women who didn't want to be tied down with a permanent relationship. He hadn't been serious with anyone since college, and while normally he prided himself on keeping his thoughts in character, he'd have to allow himself a little leeway. She wore her hair swept onto her head in a fancy knot, tendrils framing her expressive face, diamonds scattered in her shiny dark hair.

He told himself he was preparing for the grilling his sisters would give him when he got back home. While he could never reveal his missions to his family, he could eventually recount his appearance at this ball. His real sisters would want all the details. But he'd be lying to himself if he didn't admit that he was enjoying the job of accompanying and protecting the princess.

However, all he now seemed able to focus on clearly was her face. She wore makeup that emphasized her blue eyes and high cheekbones. Her full lips, taunting him with a glossy red lipstick, begged to be kissed. But it was the graceful arch of her neck that had him thinking very unbrotherly thoughts. Thoughts of nipping his way up her neck to her ear. Thoughts of kissing his way down to her collarbone. Thoughts of claiming that glossy red mouth.

Totally inappropriate thoughts. This was his first public impersonation as Alexander. He needed to concentrate and to remind himself that failure wasn't an option, since it could cost Tashya her life.

They entered the ballroom down a wide curving staircase. The ballroom, huge and lit by ornate chandeliers, was already crowded with well-dressed couples, a few elderly matrons and several bachelors and single ladies. The scent of flowers wafted to him in the air along with a multitude of languages—English, Arabic, Russian and Hebrew—spoken in cultured voices. An orchestra played a lively waltz, but no one danced. Apparently Vashmiran tradition called for the king and queen to enjoy the first dance before others could follow suit.

A waiter in livery joined them as they reached the bottom of the stairs and handed them drinks, Tashya a flute of champagne and Hunter the prince's favorite Chivas Regal. He sipped, enjoying Alex's fine taste in liquor.

Tashya sipped her bubbly, her red lips leaving behind just a touch of lipstick on her glass. She surveyed the crowd as if with the specific purpose of finding someone in particular. A lover? The thought made him cringe. He didn't like the idea.

Tashya led him to several people he recognized as influential cabinet members. His tension immediately eased as he realized that this might be a ball, but the princess was using the social occasion to work the room.

"General," Hunter nodded to General Levsky Vladimir, a man in his mid-fifties with cropped gray hair, a pot belly and sharp brown eyes, who nodded a greeting. He wore a brown military dress uniform with rows of ribbons and medals across his chest, and he was eyeing Tashya with a stern expression. Hunter was happy to be mostly ignored and took the time to size up the general and then his aide, Stephan Cheslav, who was busy gazing at Sophia with masculine approval as she stood talking to a few women in another group across the room. Did every man in the castle consider himself a Lothario?

Hunter greeted the major, then spoke carefully in Alex's voice. "I heard my little brothers were found safe and sound with Nicholas and Ericka in the stable."

"Yes, Highness. They wanted Nicholas to take them for a ride."

Tashya released Hunter and slipped her hand onto the general's forearm as if she feared he might try for a quick departure. "Just the man I wanted to talk to."

Stephan's eyes flickered, and Hunter suspected he wished the princess had targeted him instead. However, the general looked mighty uncomfortable, as if anticipating the direction Tashya's conversation would take.

General Vladimir sought to put her off. "Highness, if this is about business—"

"Oh, it is," Tashya told him with a bright smile. As far as Hunter could discern, the general didn't soften at her attempt at charm. "You know several important laws regarding women in the military are coming up for a vote."

"For a review. Not a vote," the general insisted in his thick Russian accent. Apparently the man was highly trusted since he'd helped Tashya's father stage the revolution that had won Vashmira's independence from the former Soviet Union. While just last week General Vladimir's mistress of thirty years had failed in her bizarre attempt to assassinate the new queen and to install her own daughter on the throne, the general hadn't been implicated in the plot. The entire episode had been kept from the public, but the CIA had briefed Hunter about it. Since the general appeared to have been used by the woman, as had her husband, Vashmira's distinguished Secretary of State, Anton Belosova, both men had kept their important positions on the cabinet and were here tonight to honor Vashmira's new queen.

"Women make up half the population of our country, General," Tashya told him with a bold earnestness.

Hunter thought Alexander might insert into the conversation a somewhat irrelevant and sexist comment to tease his sister and added, "Our men in uniform would surely appreciate working with the ladies. I certainly do so at every opportunity."

Stephan chuckled. The general frowned.

Tashya ignored his improper comment. "Women are a valuable asset to this country and a resource we should be willing to employ."

"I'm willing," Hunter murmured.

From across the room, a beautiful blond woman winked at Hunter. He didn't recognize her from any of the pictures Tashya had shown him. But something in her eyes made him believe she knew Alexander intimately.

Trouble. She could be big trouble, Hunter thought as he continued to monitor the conversation around him, inserting shallow comments meant to annoy Tashya and to stay in character. She'd told him Alex had taken particular delight in needling her in public while secretly working to help her cause.

However, only part of his mind remained on the

conversation around him. At the first opportunity he intended to ask Tashya the blonde's identity and her relationship to Alexander.

Stephan awkwardly injected his opinion into the conversation, probably trying to impress both his boss and the princess with a reasonable-sounding argument. "We might be willing to employ women secretaries and clerks, but we don't have the funds to train women soldiers in separate facilities."

"Who said anything about separate facilities? Why not train women pilots?" Tashya pressed him. "And medics and doctors and truck drivers—"

The general shook his head. "I don't want women on the front. The Israelis tried it. And their enemies fought harder because they were ashamed to surrender to women."

Tashya's gaze shifted to a flurry of activity at the curving staircase. Doors opened. Security entered. Hunter figured that she knew the king and queen would soon make their grand entrance and sought to wind up matters quickly.

"I'd like to discuss this further next week, General. How about Monday? Say at ten o'clock?"

The general and the major exchanged discrete glances that Tashya couldn't see from her position at the general's side. Hunter suspected that when she showed up for the meeting, the general would be otherwise occupied and leave his aide to make explanations.

Hunter caught Tashya's gaze and then looked at the blonde. The princess picked up on his signal perfectly. "Alexander, don't you dare desert me for Madeline Leonid. Just because you enjoyed your frolic with her last month at the beach and are no doubt anxious to renew your acquaintance is no reason to leave me alone. Don't forget, we haven't caught the person who took potshots at us in our carriage. You promised Nicholas to stay by my side.''

Perfect. She'd handled his silent query like a professional, and just in time, as Madeline shouldered her way through the throng of people to join them. The general turned to speak to others, his aide went off to pursue Sophia, leaving Hunter with the two women.

Madeline curtsied when no one else had, showing more cleavage than necessary. She wore a little too much perfume and stunning pearls that were knotted in the spectacular cleavage revealed by a low-cut, emerald-and-gold gown. ''How good to see you again. I heard you've been ill, but you look terrific as always.''

Her husky voice and eyes said more, promising him whatever he wanted.

With a too bright smile, Madeline turned to Tashya. ''Highness, your gown is striking. Is your designer French?''

''Actually, she's Vashmiran. I like to support our country's economy whenever I can.''

''How noble. However, I cannot imagine Alex without his Versace and Armani clothes.''

Great. From the predatory gleam in Madeline's eyes, he guessed she'd been close enough to read the labels. Probably had read them as she'd ripped them off Alex's body. He had no doubts that she anticipated a repeat performance.

It wouldn't be the first time he'd disappointed a woman. Hunter didn't socialize with women while on the job—not ever. He may have turned down several terrific ladies but, on the other hand, he was still alive. And if he accomplished this mission with his usual efficiency, he could snare that Cobra assignment.

Hunter flashed Madeline Alex's charming-the-lady-of-the-moment grin. "I do so appreciate the finer things in life." The way he said the words, he meant for her to believe she was one of the finer things in his life. If Tashya had drilled one thing into him, it was how Alex acted in public. Basically, he would compliment the ladies, smile and flirt. Unfortunately, Hunter found small talk very boring, but for his royal role, he would flirt if necessary.

Apparently the general had detained Stephan, who still eyed Sophia but who apparently couldn't leave the general's side without permission. Alone, Sophia, wearing a modest-cut, bronze-colored gown and a fortune in amber stones around her neck, joined Tashya, Madeline and Hunter. "Good evening."

"Hi, Sophia." Tashya greeted her stepmother with genuine affection. "Did you get a nap this afternoon?"

It always amazed him how Tashya seemed to know so much about the people in the palace when she'd spent so much time with him. Through their many discussions, the princess had revealed her love for her family. Since her biological mother had died during the revolution, Sophia, a mere ten years older than Tashya, was the only mother she'd ever known. Tashya worried about her older brothers and enjoyed playing with the little ones and holding the baby.

"I did catch a nap, but the boys evaded their guards and their nanny. They turned up in the stable. Again. Apparently, the guards found them after they watched a foal being born."

Alex nodded his approval. "A fine way for them to learn about...life."

"Easy for you to say. You didn't have to answer their innumerable questions."

Clearly, Madeline had no interest in children, but she wasn't about to give up her spot beside Hunter. He wondered if she intended to cling to him all evening. But when a slender brunette with a come-hither expression caught his eye, Madeline leaned toward him, revealing her cleavage again.

If Tashya or Sophia were aware of Madeline's overt move, they didn't indicate it. Hunter yearned to slap her hand away or to at least change position and break the physical contact. But Alex would probably enjoy this kind of relentless pursuit.

Finally the king and queen made their appearance. Nicholas wore a tuxedo and a proud smile as he presented his new bride, who wore a stunning lace gown, to the approving crowd. The chatter in the ballroom ceased as all eyes turned to the loving couple.

When they reached the ballroom floor, the orchestra struck up a Hungarian melody. Nicholas took Ericka into his arms, his expression so tender that it brought tears to many a lady's eyes. Guests moved back, clearing a space as he twirled her around the room.

Hunter could no longer stand Madeline's questing hand. He broke contact and whispered in her ear. "I'm sorry, the next dance is promised to my sister."

Madeline's eyes narrowed in disappointment, but she kept her tone light. "And the dance after that?"

Hunter told himself Alex would not refuse this woman, but then he wouldn't allow himself to remain with one lady for the evening when there were so many beautiful women waiting to dance with him. He disengaged from her with a simple, "Find me later."

She made no effort to keep her voice low. "Count on it, darling."

Her words made him feel as if he needed a shower. He had no intention of being available to Madeline. As the king and queen's dance ended and another began, he took a surprised Tashya into his arms. She covered well, not even missing a step.

"I've never before felt like a piece of meat," he admitted under the cover of the music.

She giggled. "Alex enjoys the game."

She could at least sound the slightest bit jealous. Didn't she notice that every single woman in the room between eighteen and eighty seemed to be trying to catch his eye? But then, there were plenty of men giving their princess that same kind of attention, too.

Tashya seemed oblivious to the admiration of the men. Now he understood the true meaning of the phrase "living in a fishbowl."

It was a wonder Nicholas had managed to fall in love under such circumstances. For the king and queen, the pressures had to be even worse. Add the occasional assassination attempt to the mix, never mind constant scrutiny by the press, and Hunter realized they were doing well to avoid the need for therapy.

Tashya danced in his arms, adjusting to his steps with an ease that indicated she'd been partnered by many men. She looked up at him, her expression mischievous. "Madeline's just waiting for this dance to end so that she can reclaim you."

"It's not funny."

"Or if you prefer, there's a redhead over there in a rhinestone dress trying to win your attention."

Having spotted the overdressed schoolgirl earlier, he didn't bother to look. "She can't be of legal age. Surely, Alex didn't—?"

"He rarely misses an opportunity to flirt. But he does seem to prefer them over twenty-one."

The tune ended all too soon. Again Hunter felt a hand groping him. He looked down and spied the two little princes, who had evaded their nanny once more. Tashya's and Alex's half brothers weren't dressed for the ball and had obviously sneaked in to watch the adult activities. Where were their guards? Where was the nanny?

Hunter recalled from an earlier conversation with Tashya that Sophia's royal duties during the day required a nanny to watch the boys and the baby. At night, the nanny went home and Sophia took over, wanting to be a hands-on mom. Tonight, with Sophia at the ball, the nanny had agreed to spend the night with her charges and should have kept them under close supervision.

The music ended. Couples stopped dancing and broke apart. Before people resumed their conversations, there was a moment of silence.

Hunter leaned down toward the boys, but the bigger child took a suspicious step back. Dimitri frowned at him, his serious face puckered in distrust, his eyes full of wariness. Clearly the boy had suspicions about Hunter's identity.

At the sight of Dimitri's expression, Tashya paled and held out her arms to the child, who ignored her Dimitri continued to stare at Hunter with observant eyes.

Hunter scooped Nikita onto his hip, glad of the hours he'd spent with his nieces and nephews back home. "Dimitri. Niki. What are you boys doing here?"

Dimitri lifted his five-year-old head, pointed straight at Hunter's heart and loudly proclaimed, "He's not Alex. He's a fake."

Chapter Five

Oh...my...God. Stunned silence swept across the room. Necks craned in their direction.

Tashya felt the blood drain from her head. Never in her darkest nightmare had she dreamed that Dimitri would show up and accuse Hunter of being an imposter. He'd fooled security, old girlfriends, Sophia, General Vladimir and Major Cheslav; yet a five-year-old now accused him of impersonating Alex.

Hunter didn't miss a beat. "Of course I'm an imposter, Dimitri. I'm really James Bond in disguise."

Several people chuckled, and the tension eased as the music restarted. Most couples either returned to their dancing or their conversations and drinks. Obviously the guests believed Hunter was the real Prince Alexander and was playing games with Dimitri. With quick wit, Hunter had turned the situation from a disaster to a minor problem.

Still, Tashya found herself holding her breath, fascinated and waiting to see what outrageous thing Hunter would say next. Never had she expected him to admit the very thing he was trying to hide. The man was brilliant.

Hunter ignored the few people still paying attention

to his conversation with Dimitri and held out his hand to her still suspicious but nevertheless fascinated little brother. "My mission is to guard the princess. You mustn't give me away."

Dimitri frowned. "I just did."

"But we're among friends, and they won't tell." Hunter glanced her way. "However, someone's going to think *Tashya* is pretending to be the princess if *she* doesn't relax. You gave our sister quite a scare."

Sophia hurried over, Major Stephan Cheslav trailing her. Tashya had seen the them dancing together earlier and wondered if romance might be in the air. Sophia had truly loved King Zared I and had mourned his loss deeply, but she was still young, full of life. Tashya approved of the new sparkle in her stepmother's eyes—although Tashya couldn't tell whether Stephan or her mischievous children had put it there.

"Alex, I'm *so* sorry," Sophia apologized with a shake of her head. She glared at her naughty sons, but her expression lost some of the sting when her lips broke into a slight smile. "My children are supposed to be in bed."

"But coming to the dance is so much more fun." Hunter winked at Nikita on his hip and the three-year-old chuckled, probably relieved he wasn't in bad trouble.

Sophia reached for Nikita, but Hunter didn't hand him over. "I'll put them to bed."

Alex wouldn't have made that offer. Her brother enjoyed flirting and dancing too much to miss a party—even for a few minutes. His offhand remark caused Sophia's eyes to widen just a bit.

Tashya quickly leaned forward and lowered her

voice so only Sophia and Hunter could hear, "Alex is doing his best to avoid a certain blonde. Especially since he's made plans to meet with a redhead."

Indeed, as they spoke, Madeline bore down on him like a heat-seeking missile, giving credence to Tashya's lie.

Stephan held out his hand to Sophia. "How about another dance?"

"Give me a minute." Sophia kissed Nikita, then Dimitri. "You boys go with Tashya and Alex."

"James Bond," Dimitri insisted.

Sophia ruffled her son's dark hair and straightened his pajama top. "If you say so, dear."

Tashya took Dimitri by the hand and followed Hunter as he carried Nikita through the crowd, narrowly avoiding Madeline. With unerring accuracy, Hunter strode through the hallways, talking with the children, fully aware that he and Tashya couldn't speak freely until they reached Alex's private apartments.

The children, Tashya and Hunter entered Sophia's suite, and their nanny rushed over to them, concern and relief in her eyes. The pretty woman's eyes looked as if she'd been crying, her nose red. Tashya knew Sophia had checked Neve's background thoroughly before hiring her. Most importantly, Neve loved the two little boys.

Neve sniffled. "Highness, I went to the bathroom, and the next thing I knew, they were gone. I'm really very responsible—" a little frustration entered her tone "—but with these two imps a girl needs eyes in the back of her head."

"It's all right," Hunter told her kindly.

"They slip away from Sophia all the time," Tashya

added. She couldn't help recalling the mischief she, Nicholas and Alexander had gotten into when they were children. Their father had usually found the three of them in the stable, feeding the horses or napping in the hayloft.

"Nikita's practically asleep." Hunter handed Nikita to the nanny. "The little guy is all tuckered out. If you'll put him to bed, we'll do the same for Dimitri."

"Thank you, Highness."

Tashya suspected Hunter wanted a private word with Dimitri. Still, she didn't expect him to be so direct.

As soon as the nanny was out of earshot, Hunter bent until he could look Dimitri in the eyes. "May I ask what gave me away?"

"You look like Alex, but you don't dance like him," Dimitri told him.

"I don't, hmm?"

Hunter stood, took Tashya into his arms and twirled her around. Surprised at his sudden playfulness, she went along with his dance. But Hunter's attention focused on a frowning Dimitri. "What am I doing wrong?"

"I don't know."

Hunter stopped in mid-stride and steadied her. "It's all right, Dimitri. You're very observant."

"What's that mean?"

"You see things other people don't."

"Oh. Other people don't look."

Hunter and Tashya exchanged a glance. His was, *I told you so.* Hers said, *Now what?*

Talk about the truth coming out of the mouths of

babes... Dimitri was one smart little boy. Sending him away was not an option.

"Where's Alex?" Dimitri asked.

"Nicholas sent him to the United States of America," Tashya explained. "I couldn't go because I have work to do here."

"And I'm pretending to be Alex so that I can protect Tashya."

"But we have guards."

"The guards don't go in the private areas. I do," Hunter explained simply and concisely. "And only Nicholas, Tashya and I know that I'm not Alex."

"You want me to keep it a secret?" Dimitri asked, far too wise for his years.

"It would be for the best if you just didn't talk about me at all," Hunter suggested.

"What about my mother?" Dimitri asked.

Tashya sighed. "We already know you don't tell Sophia everything."

"Do, too," Dimitri insisted.

"So she knows about the kitten you sneak from the stable into bed every night?" Tashya asked him with a smile.

Dimitri climbed into bed, reached under the blanket and pulled the kitten onto his chest. He petted her gently until she purred. "She's a secret."

"And I'm a secret, too." Hunter tucked the blanket around him. "Okay?"

Dimitri nodded. "Okay."

"Thank you," Hunter told him, seemingly not the least bit worried that his life could at any time be placed at risk by a five-year-old.

TASHYA HAD NO opportunity to speak privately with Hunter until hours later after the ball had ended. Time and again, he'd successfully eluded Madeline, never dancing twice with the same woman. He'd played the part of Alex with supreme confidence, dancing, flirting as if he'd never done anything else during his entire life, but never allowing a woman to corner him into a private tête-à-tête.

Back in Alex's quarters, away from the guards, away from the matchmaking mothers and pursuing women, they seemed once again cloaked in a cocoon of privacy. Almost as if they'd gone to the dance as a couple and had planned to meet afterward. She knew the notion was silly, yet she couldn't shake the feeling of intimacy between them, wasn't even sure if she wanted to. Perhaps her feelings were simply a natural result of their growing closeness. At times she'd thought she could read his mind—but at others, he'd totally surprised her.

She started to discuss the question that had nagged her ever since Dimitri had spied him for a fake. "I think—"

Hunter raised a finger to his lips, took a device from his belongings and slowly walked through the suite, holding the instrument in front of him. "It's clean."

She frowned, wondering if he felt the tension, too, and was walking away to put some distance between them. "Alex's valet cleans up every time Alex steps out the door."

"I meant, there are no bugs. No electronic listening devices were planted during our absence."

She should have known he would stick to business. The attraction and admiration she'd begun to feel toward him was no doubt one-sided. "So it's safe to speak?"

"Go ahead."

She looked him straight in the eyes. "I think you should quit."

"Why?" He hitched up his slacks just as Alexander did before he sat beside her on the sofa, and continued to speak to her in the prince's voice. She supposed staying in character was easier for him, but she missed his American accent.

She sighed. "We can't depend on my five-year-old brother to keep such a big secret."

Hunter carelessly ran his fingers through his hair, messing up his Alex look. "Even if he decides to talk, who's going to believe him?"

She hadn't thought of that. Was she simply looking for an excuse for him to leave before she became any more intrigued with him? Although she'd always wanted to marry someday, Hunter wasn't marriage material. She knew that and perhaps not so unconsciously she was seeking to protect herself from eventual pain.

"What I'm more concerned about is the meetings you set up for next week. Perhaps you should consider canceling them." Hunter placed his arm over the back of the sofa, relaxing. If she leaned back, she would be in his embrace.

"Why?" Tashya stiffened her spine, not leaning back in the slightest. "We still don't know if the same person who shot at Alex and me in the carriage is the same person who sent that bomb. We don't know if the target is me, Alex, or both of us. I don't suppose you saw anything suspicious tonight?"

"Almost everything I saw was suspicious, Princess.'' He said the words in a sexy drawl that made her heart reach out to him. What kind of world did he live in that he never let down his guard, never trusted anyone?

She'd asked him not to call her princess, and yet somehow, on his lips, the words sounded almost like an endearment. ''What did I miss?''

He ticked off points, one by one. ''General Vladimir whispering in Stephan's ear.''

''Stephan works for the general. I hardly see anything sinister.''

''So why did they hide behind the potted plants?''

Okay. ''What else?''

''Sophia and Stephan's sudden friendship.''

He viewed a budding romance as suspicious? ''And why is that suspect?''

''Because as the mother of the royal princes, Sophia has the most to gain from Nicholas's, Alex's and your deaths. Maybe she's plotting for her sons to inherit. Since she probably would need help making a bomb...and since Stephan is in the military...''

Tashya couldn't imagine the gentle Sophia engaging in a love affair so she could get help in making a bomb. But Tashya had no facts to back up her intuition, and she already knew Hunter was a man who needed facts. Sometimes he acted as if he didn't have feelings, but at other times he was kind and warm, as he had been with Dimitri. Clearly he liked children. ''What else?''

''Ira Hanuck, your security chief, didn't show his face all evening.''

''Maybe you just didn't *see* him.''

''He wasn't there.''

Hunter's confidence amazed her. How had he noticed all these details when he'd been so busy impersonating Alex, dancing and conversing? "If Ira *had* showed up, would that have been suspicious, too?"

Hunter shrugged, a very puzzling shrug.

"Who else?"

"The nanny."

"What about *Neve?*"

"She didn't even ask where we found the boys."

"And that is suspicious because…"

"Because it was a normal question and she missed it."

Tashya rolled her eyes at the ceiling. "You are too much. Next you'll be telling me that Nicholas and Ericka—"

"Besides your little brothers, the king and queen were the only people in the room I don't suspect."

"Because they have nothing to gain by Alex's and my deaths?"

"Exactly."

"Wait a minute." She frowned at him. "You didn't mention my name among the people you don't suspect."

He grinned, placed his arm across her shoulders and tilted her back against the sofa. "Ah, I thought you might catch that."

The warmth from his arm around her shoulders contrasted with the coolness of his words. She swallowed hard and forced her tone to remain calm although her pulse raced. "You suspect me?"

"I can't eliminate you from the list."

Was he insane? She twisted out from under his arm and faced him. "What are you saying? I'm the one whose life is in danger here."

"But maybe you're trying to kill Alex. What better

way to look innocent than to claim that you're in danger, too?''

''So I sent myself a bomb? After I knew Alex was gone? That makes no sense.''

''Unless you want to make yourself look innocent in my eyes.''

She glared at him. ''And why in hell would I care what you think?'' Even as she asked the question, she knew she did care what he thought. Insulted, angry, hurt, she leapt to her feet. ''You are one twisted piece of work.''

''THIS ISN'T GOING the way I planned,'' Hunter admitted softly.

''What?''

''Deliberately making you angry isn't supposed to make *me* feel like a heel.''

''Deliberately?'' She crossed her arms over her chest. ''You wanted me angry? Why?''

''I need a clear head to do my job properly—''

''You decided to make me angry...so I'd push you away.'' Her voice dropped to a whisper.

''I'm not good at apologies, but I owe you one, Princess.'' He looked up at her from his position on the sofa. ''I was wrong to even imply that you could kill anyone—especially family. After listening to you speak so fondly of Alex for hours, after seeing how much you care for Nicholas, Ericka, Sophia, Dimitri and Nikita, I know you could never plan their murders. I'm sorry.'' He ran his fingers through his hair again. ''But understand that someone is after you. It's my job to protect you, and I need to think about work. Not about kissing you.''

''You...want...to...kiss me?''

He had no idea what she was thinking, but her pupils dilated until he could see only a thin ring of blue. The arch of her neck revealed her racing pulse, and he wondered if she considered him an unfeeling bastard for trying to manipulate her. If someone had treated one of his sisters as badly as he'd just treated her, he would have had a difficult time restraining his anger.

Remorse and pain knotted in his gut. Damn it. He was a professional. He knew better than to let himself become emotionally involved while on a mission. It was bad enough that he'd let himself become distracted, but he'd caused her pain just because he feared that if he allowed her to remain close, he would lose control, maybe kiss her. Definitely kiss her.

Even now, he didn't dare stand and put himself within arm's reach. Every cell in his body ached to gather her into his arms, soothe away the pain he'd caused. Through gritted teeth, he spoke gruffly. "You should go."

"I do not think so." Her words, spoken softly, held a hint of tension that made his hopes leap.

He squashed them flat.

"I want you, Princess. Believe me when I tell you that right now I can think about only one thing."

"What?"

"Making love to you." He dug his fingers into his bunched thighs, determined not to budge, wishing she'd go before he made a move he'd regret.

"I'm not a coward. You don't scare me. Despite what you say, you wouldn't force an unwilling woman."

"True. But we both know that you're *not* unwilling." He drilled her with a stare that had often made battle-scarred men retreat. "And we both know you aren't the kind of woman who enjoys a fling. There's no future for us, Princess."

"We have now."

Reaching down, she took his hand, tugged him to his feet. Within a moment he held her in his arms. Held her close enough to feel her heart thudding against his chest. Held her close enough to know that kissing her wouldn't be enough.

Dipping his head, until his lips barely caressed hers, he gave her one last chance to run. "You sure?"

She placed her forearm on his shoulder, dragged his head down. "I've never been *less* sure in my life. But sometimes, I go on instinct."

"And what are those instincts telling you, Princess?"

"That this kiss is going to be...unforgettable."

As her words shimmied under his skin, they showered him with a warm glow, and he vowed to give her a kiss so unforgettable it couldn't fail to live up to her expectations.

However, not even he could have anticipated the thrumming urgency that possessed him. She tasted like the finest champagne, intoxicating his blood, firing his senses and inflaming his yearnings. Under his nipping persuasion, she parted her lips, welcoming him into her warmth, holding him as if she had no intention of ever letting him go.

They had all night. He needn't rush.

But he already felt revved to full speed, his senses demanding more. His princess sure knew how to give a kiss, a royal kiss.

Hungry for more, but starving for air, he broke his mouth from hers to seize a ragged breath. She gave him only one breath and then their mouths fused back together, creating heavenly sensations.

A pounding noise slowly permeated his consciousness. Pounding at Alex's front door.

Hunter placed his hands on Tashya's shoulder, watched her eyes slowly focus. "Something's wrong."

He drew his weapon but held it out of sight as palace security swooped into the room. Sophia hurried in right behind them, her face streaked with tears, a piece of paper in her hand.

"What's wrong?" Tashya asked, recovering from their kiss with seeming ease.

Sophia thrust the paper at her.

Hunter discretely tucked away his weapon and read the paper over Tashya's shoulder. Words had been cut from a newspaper and glued to the kidnapping demand.

Dimitri and Nikita are with me. If you want to see them alive, Alexander and Tashya must go to the front entrance to the National Museum. Come alone. Immediately. I am watching. Delay will not be tolerated.

"Oh, God." Tashya dropped the paper and hugged the sobbing Sophia. "We'll get them back. Don't worry. Alex and I will do whatever is necessary."

Hunter spoke to the guards with Alex's authority. "Who else knows the boys are missing?"

"No one, Highness."

"You are to tell no one, but search the palace for any sign of them yourselves and report back to Nicholas or me. Do you understand?"

"Yes, Highness." He waved the guards away, hoping they wouldn't contact anyone, not even the security chief, whom he still didn't trust.

"Tashya, Sophia." Hunter sharpened his voice to get their attention. "I need to speak with the nanny."

"Neve's mother is in the hospital. I sent her home around midnight so she could visit her first thing in the morning," Sophia told him. "The boys disappeared in the last hour."

"How do you know?" he asked.

"Nikita had a nightmare at 1:00 a.m. I comforted him."

Hunter checked his watch. It was ten after two. "What about the security cameras? Isn't there one always on the boys' room?"

"Ira's checking it for me," Sophia told him.

Damn. He supposed it had been too much to ask that the security chief could remain uninformed. But now that he had been brought into this mess, Ira might be of some use. "Sophia, Ira will need to question Neve and the guards on duty."

Speak of the security chief. Ira Hanuck, with King Nicholas and Queen Ericka, strode through Alex's apartment. All their faces were grim.

"I've checked the security tape," Ira told Hunter, obviously having overheard the tail end of their conversation. "Someone looped it."

"Looped?" Tashya asked.

Hunter had to be careful to stay in character while his mind raced over options for his next move. He didn't know if Alex was familiar with the term "loop" and left the explanation to Ira.

"They taped footage of the boys while they slept, then had the camera repeatedly replay that segment.

To the guard monitoring the tape, everything looked normal.''

''He thought the boys were still in bed?'' Sophia asked.

''The four cameras covering that hallway were all looped. The children's guards were told over their radios to report to the main gatehouse. Whoever gave that order knew the correct password. The guards obeyed.''

Hunter, careful to mimic the prince, had to speak up since no one had mentioned Sophia's third child. ''Make sure another guard is placed on the baby immediately.''

Ira nodded, bent and picked up the note with tweezers he extracted from a pocket. ''We'll analyze this for prints, check the glue, and see if we can discover which newspaper the words were cut from.''

Hunter spoke in Alex's voice. ''Tashya and I need to pack.''

''Why?'' Tashya asked.

''This may take longer than a few hours.'' He didn't want to say more in front of the others, but he suspected the kidnappers might lead them on from one location to another. ''We should probably go within the next ten minutes, or we may make the kidnappers think that we aren't coming.''

King Nicholas took Hunter's arm, led him into Alex's bedroom and shut the door. ''You're taking Tashya with you?''

''The kidnappers have left me no choice. There's no time to find her a double, Your Majesty.'' Hunter thrust several of Alex's shirts into a bag along with jeans and socks. He searched for underwear, then recalled that the prince didn't wear any, an item he'd never have let slip his mind if he hadn't already been so concerned over taking an untrained woman, a civilian, on a dangerous mission.

Nicholas frowned. "You can't guarantee my sister's safety, can you?"

"I don't make promises I can't keep." Hunter savagely zipped the duffel. "However, I assure you that I will do my best to protect her."

"I'm not sure I should allow you to take Tashya into danger. You could all be killed."

"But we may save the kids and survive." Hunter saw the indecision on Nicholas's face. "I've been in worse spots, Your Majesty."

"Take this." Nicholas handed him a thick envelope stuffed with cash.

Without counting, Hunter estimated and roughly divided the money into thirds. One third he tucked into a money belt, one third he shoved into his wallet, and the last he jammed deep into his duffel. He always kept the duffel fully stocked with essentials and packed to go on a moment's notice. Inside were tools of the trade, tools he could do without if necessary, but experience told him they would come in handy.

"Before you arrived, I sent two guards to search the palace to make sure the kids aren't still here. I instructed them to report to you."

Nicholas nodded. "If we find them, you'll be the first person I call."

Since Tashya had already stated her willingness to help, they'd best move quickly. Hunter swung the duffel over his shoulder, his heart heavy with the knowledge that he was most surely leading Tashya into a trap. A trap that could get them all killed.

Chapter Six

While Hunter had spoken to Nicholas, Tashya's maid had packed her a backpack with toiletries and clothing. Tashya had changed into jeans, a shirt, sneakers and a denim jacket that would not only keep her warm but also help her to blend in with the tourists who vacationed in Vashmira during the summer.

Tashya hugged Nicholas goodbye and asked Ericka to take care of Sophia, as Hunter hustled her out of the suite. She was stunned, putting one foot in front of the other automatically, her thoughts so muddled by the sudden turn of events that she couldn't seem to concentrate. First, she and Hunter had shared that fantastic kiss. The next, tragedy had struck like a lightning bolt out of a quiet sky.

That someone was using two innocent children to get to her and Alex sickened her. While she was glad Alex was safely gone, she couldn't help but worry over the rest of her family. Sophia looked as if she'd aged ten years in the last ten minutes. Nicholas had that hunted looked in his eyes again—a look that he'd worn for months after their father's death and that Ericka had banished.

They had to find the boys quickly. She couldn't

even imagine how terrified they would be to find themselves among strangers. They might be precocious, but they were loved and pampered, too. Sick at heart, she wished she could think clearly. They'd been up for hours, but resting wasn't possible. Neither was escaping the iciness that gripped her with nightmarish tentacles. She'd never felt so scared in her life. Her palms were clammy. She couldn't drag enough oxygen into her starving lungs. Nausea rose from her stomach up into her throat. Despite her jacket, she couldn't seem to get warm.

While she would trade her life to save Dimitri and Nikita, the rational side of her doubted that any of them would come out of this venture alive. She didn't need Hunter to point out the obvious to her; they were walking into a trap.

However, she couldn't live with herself if she didn't try to get the boys back. She would do her very best. Then she would do more.

To outsiders, Princess Tashya might have led a sheltered life, but she'd had to overcome much adversity during the previous two and a half decades. As a small child she'd lost her mother and, last year, she'd lost her father. While she could call upon both emotional strength—hard won from overcoming the losses of parents she'd loved—and physical strength—developed by riding and training horses—she worried that she might not be able to keep up with Hunter.

He was the ace in the hole. The kidnapper expected Alex, not a trained military strategist, or spy, or CIA agent, or whatever the hell he was. Since the information was classified, she didn't know which branch of the United States' government Hunter worked for, but it didn't matter. All their lives rested on his ability. She couldn't slow him down. Even if her knees felt like water, she would walk. If she felt terror, she would swallow it. She had to be strong, for Sophia, for the boys, for Hunter.

When Hunter gripped her arm and steered her through a side door of the palace, she stiffened her resolve. Outside the protective stone walls that two thousand years ago had surrounded an entire city and protected the populace, it appeared an ordinary summer night. The occasional dog barked. A balmy breeze brushed her hair. The scent of freshly mowed grasses teased her nostrils, and the crescent moon played peek-a-boo with scudding clouds.

Beside her, Hunter whispered. "Nicholas arranged for us to use an armored car. It's parked across the street."

The gray sedan must have come from the motor pool. Tashya didn't know if she felt more exposed crossing the street or more of a target once inside the vehicle. Hunter turned off the car's interior light. She strapped herself into the passenger seat, wondering how long the armored car could protect them.

She clasped her hands together. "I feel as if someone's watching us."

"Two someones." Hunter started the engine. "Ira will have ordered a palace security guard to follow us. He may also have planted a tracking device on this car."

"Why do you say that?"

"Because in his position, that's what I would do."

She shook her head. "Nicholas wouldn't have allowed Ira to risk it."

"Nicholas may not know."

Hunter took his time, driving slowly through mostly deserted city streets toward the National Museum. They passed a newspaper delivery truck and a fuel tanker. At this late hour, every shop was closed. Even the pubs had shut down by 2:00 a.m.

Hunter's voice was calm. "The second tail is military."

"How can you tell?"

"His erect bearing is a dead giveaway. The man's a rank amateur. Whether or not he's been sent by the children's kidnapper is another question. How're you holding up?"

He shifted topics on her quickly, but she still had time to make up a lie. "I'm fine."

Obviously she wasn't, and he knew it. "It's okay to be scared. Scared makes the adrenaline gush. Adrenaline keeps you alert. That's why you thought someone was watching us. Your subconscious picked up the tails."

He might be trying to reassure her, but he wasn't succeeding. Although she knew she wouldn't see anything suspicious, she had the strongest urge to look behind her. She had to force herself not to turn to glance over her shoulder. Without being told, even she realized that giving away their knowledge of their tails would be foolish.

"What worries me is the tails you don't see."

"That's an optimistic thought." He didn't seem the least perturbed that she'd openly questioned his ability. In fact, he almost seemed pleased that she didn't relax.

"What's your plan?" she asked him, wondering how he could be so calm. She supposed that to him this kind of mission was old hat. Was he one of those men who didn't feel alive until he risked his life? Did he live for the adrenaline rush like a race car driver addicted to speed, or a mountain climber always in search of a more difficult climb?

Hunter spoke in an offhand manner. "The mission is simple. We rescue the kids. Put the kidnapper behind bars."

"Just how are we going to find the kids?" she asked softly.

"I have no idea."

"You're joking, right?"

"I'm afraid not."

She bit back a gasp. She'd expected him to tell her what to do, how to react, what to say. "What do you mean, you have no plan?"

"We don't know what will happen after we reach the museum, so planning's impossible."

She had thought that the kidnapper would be waiting at the museum for them. But she realized that wouldn't be smart. Nicholas could send a contingent of police to surround the museum, and the kidnapper would be trapped.

Somehow she'd assumed that one way or another, whatever happened would occur within the next hour. *Idiot.* Hunter had told her to pack clothes almost immediately after reading the kidnapper's note. He'd suspected right from the start that this mission could last longer than tonight.

As the moon peeked out from behind a cloud, she prayed for courage. Prayed that when the time came, she would do what had to be done. Prayed that she wouldn't let the boys or Hunter down.

Hunter drove right past the National Museum, a three-story gray building with soaring columns and wide stairs that led up to solid-looking front doors flanked by urns stolen by the Ottomans. As they drove by, she didn't see anyone. No suspicious cars. No one lurking in the bushes. Nothing.

"You're going to park?" she asked.

He pulled an illegal U-turn. "By the pay phone."

She hadn't noted the phone booth at the bottom of the stairs until he'd mentioned it. "Why?"

"Just a hunch."

He parked the car, then reached into his duffel bag and extracted a square device with a keypad and several dangling wires. Before she could ask one question, he unfastened his seat belt and exited the car.

He spoke to her through the open door. "Lock the car behind me. Don't get out. If there's trouble, drive away. You do know how to drive?"

"Yes." But she didn't drive well. Although she had a valid driver's license, she didn't often practice. Her driver usually chauffeured her through the busy streets in the limousine.

As Hunter straightened, the phone in the booth rang. Without haste, as if he'd expected the call, he strode around the car, keeping the odd-looking device hidden in shadows.

The phone rang again.

Hurry, Hunter. Answer it.

He didn't rush. Instead he cracked open the phone booth door just enough to smash the overhead light before it illuminated him. Made him a target.

Again, the phone rang.

Reaching under the return coin slot, he jacked in a wire and attached the keypad device to the receiver. He carefully ran his fingers along the seat and under it, checking for...explosives maybe?

Finally he picked up the ringing phone.

From inside the protection of the armored car, she couldn't hear what he was saying. But she was so focused on him that she didn't notice the three men until they were only a few steps away.

One man tried to jerk open her car door. The heavy-plated door with security locks didn't budge. But her breath hitched, and the nausea in her tummy burned. Hunter was out there, outnumbered three to one.

In the blink of an eye, Hunter left the phone dangling off the hook and escaped the limited confines of the phone booth. As one man slashed with his knife, Hunter smoothly shifted out of the line of attack, grabbed his foe's wrist and twisted the weapon loose, then slammed the off balance man's head into the corner of the phone booth.

Hunter released his grip on the downed man in time to take on a second one. His movements a blur of speed and grace, he fought with a combination of kicks and punches until his foe lost his club and tackled him. The men grappled and tumbled to the sidewalk.

The third man tried to smash her window with a tire jack. But the special glass held. Seeing that his actions against the car were futile, her foe turned his attention and the tire iron to Hunter and his opponent.

He could kill Hunter with one blow from the tire iron. She had to do something. Act.

Without hesitation Tashya unlocked and pushed open her door, slamming it into his body. He yelped, fell with a thud and dropped the tire iron, the weapon clanging as it rolled across the pavement.

Should she pick up the tire iron?

Hunter, mimicking the sound of Alex's voice, shouted, "Get back in the car," as he rolled out from under his opponent.

He must truly have eyes in the back of his head to be able to fight someone and keep track of her at the same time—all while remembering to stay in character.

Hunter waited until Tashya slammed home the lock, then checked on the man she'd clipped with the door to ensure he wasn't going to rise back to his feet. Gesturing for her to stay put, he relieved the downed men of their weapons and wallets.

"Pop the trunk," he mouthed, then motioned what he wanted.

She found the button, pushed it, then watched him place all three men into the trunk. A normal car would never have held three men, but everything on the armored vehicle was oversize.

Finally, Hunter retrieved his phone device and got back into the car. He placed his electronic device between them on the seat. He wasn't even out of breath. "I told you not to open the door for any reason." His cool tone told her he wasn't pleased by her actions.

Too damn bad. She hardly intended to sit in safety while someone bashed in his hard head—even if he wasn't appreciative.

"You said to lock the door. I did. You said not to get out. I didn't."

"And I said, if there was any trouble, you were to drive away."

"I never agreed to that."

"Do you think we're having a debate in the Vashmiran cabinet? When I give you an order, you will follow it, Princess."

"Of course I will." *As long as I think it's the correct order.*

Tashya had spent a lot of time around strong-willed men. She found agreeing with them, then doing whatever the hell she wanted was much easier than arguing with a male loaded to the gills with testosterone. "I was about to drive away like you suggested—"

"It wasn't a suggestion—"

"—but then that man gave up on smashing the car into smithereens and targeted you instead. I just got scared and—"

"Decided to save me?" he asked wryly.

"Why, no, I was trying to save the tire iron," she muttered sarcastically. Now that they were once again more or less safe, disappointment and frustration set in. So did the shakes. They hadn't even seen Dimitri or Nikita and were no closer to finding them. "I thought the tire iron might thank me for my effort. Obviously I was mistaken."

"I appreciate the thought, but I didn't need help."

"Of course you didn't," she agreed. "Your head is much too hard to crack. Why, I'm thinking you don't even bleed."

"I could have taken out each of those men with one blow, but I'm a prince, remember?"

"I didn't know you could fight like that."

A thud in the trunk reminded her of the prisoners he'd taken. She was glad he hadn't killed them. The thought sickened her, and although she knew she was being a weak, squeamish woman, she'd never seen anyone die and had no wish to witness such violence. "Are we going to question them?"

Hunter started the engine. "There's no time. When

I answered the phone, the kidnapper instructed me to drive to the park next.''

A car swung onto the road directly behind them. Tashya picked up the lights in her side-view mirror. ''Our tails are still with us.'' If they had been sent by the military and/or palace security as Hunter had suggested, why hadn't they helped during the fracas? Instead they'd stayed back and watched Hunter handle those men, fight with a ruthless skill Alex didn't have. But would whoever had been watching know that? Had Hunter blown his impersonation of the prince?

Another thought came fast and hard-hitting. Since the kidnapper had given Hunter instructions, was the kidnapper oblivious to the attack? Or had the call been a setup to distract Hunter from the danger to make him open to attack? Or were they dealing with more than one group? ''I'm confused. Who are those men who attacked us?''

''They may or may not be connected to the kidnapper.'' He checked his watch, then dialed a number on his cell phone.

''Who are you calling?''

''The cops. We have just enough extra time to drop the men off at the police station.''

''But—''

''We don't have time to question them. Besides, they probably either won't talk or won't know anything. We have a more serious problem to discuss.''

''We do?''

He turned the radio up so high her ears hurt. Then he whispered, ''There's a chance this car may be bugged. Be careful what you say and how loudly you say it.''

''Okay.''

"I traced the kidnapper's call," he whispered.

She pointed to the keypad. "With that?"

"Yeah. I couldn't pinpoint the kidnapper's exact location because he didn't—"

"He?"

"The voice was disguised. It could have been a he or a she. He spoke educated English. No accent," he continued without pausing while the radio music camouflaged his words. "As I was saying, while I couldn't pinpoint the kidnapper's exact location because he didn't stay on the line long enough, I know that the call didn't come from the park."

"But after the police station, we're going there?"

"We have no choice. Unless you want to turn back?"

At least she could answer that particular question. "Not until we have Dimitri and Nikita."

HUNTER DIDN'T LIKE discussing the situation with Tashya, even with the radio loud enough to drown out their conversation. Normally he worked alone and had only himself to worry about. Protecting the princess complicated the mission and limited his options. Yet he couldn't leave Tashya behind—not when there was a chance the kidnapper might still exchange the kids for the prince and princess.

He would have preferred to have ditched this car, which likely had a tracing device attached to the chassis. For all he knew, Ira was back at the palace pinpointing their exact location for the kidnapper. Yet his princess was safest in the armored car.

His princess? When had he started thinking of her as anything but his responsibility? Since that spectacular kiss? Just the memory heated him. But right now, he couldn't afford any distractions. Lives were at stake.

Hunter fully believed the children were still alive, but he doubted the kidnapper's intention to eventually free the kids. That attack at the phone booth had likely been an attempt by the kidnapper to strike the prince and princess down while they were out in the open and exposed. To answer the phone, he'd had to leave the protection of the vehicle, and while he spoke to the kidnapper, he'd been attacked. The weapons they'd employed proved they'd wanted to kill them— not subdue them and lead them to the children.

Tashya was too smart not to put the pieces together. Keeping her in the dark was no longer an option.

When another song blasted over the radio, he spoke. "We have to assume the kidnapper tried to take us out at the phone booth."

"Which means he has no intention of freeing Dimitri and Nikita," she said softly.

"Probably. At some point, we'll have to decide whether to obey the kidnapper's instructions or risk going after the kids. Right now, it's not an option."

"Then why bring it up?"

"Because, Princess," he said gently, "it's going to be the most difficult decision you'll ever have to make."

She remained silent, thinking, adjusting and adapting, he hoped, to the new information. He had to give her credit, she was holding up well under the pressure.

Hunter pulled into the police parking lot and honked his horn. Two officers ambled out. When they recognized His Royal Highness, Prince Alexander of Vashmira, their sleepy demeanors sharpened, their steps quickened.

The officer in charge asked, "What can we do for you, Highness?"

Alex popped the trunk, then motioned the officers over. "These men attacked me in front of the National Museum. I want them questioned. After you run back background checks and interrogate them, I'd appreciate a phone call."

"Yes, Highness."

As Hunter got back behind the wheel, he realized there were some advantages in being recognized as the prince of Vashmira. If he'd been a normal citizen, he'd have been stuck at the police station for hours while the officers took a report and filled out forms. The stop had taken them only five minutes.

He drove through empty city streets. This area of the city was comprised of upscale stores that sold luxury merchandise. Grass along the sidewalks was neatly trimmed, and garbage cans lined up by the curb for morning pickup had fitted lids. A city block of stores and a park with a fountain defined a central square right smack in the middle of the shopping district.

"Is this the park where Nicholas and Ericka had difficulties?" Hunter asked, masking his words with a radio advertisement for cereal.

"Yes. They had to hide in the park fountain to avoid being run over by a driver. Why?"

"It could be just a coincidence that the kidnapper told us to meet in the same place." *Maybe,* he thought.

His cell phone rang. Hunter stopped the car, turned down the radio and attached the tracer, then picked up his phone. "Yes?"

"You're late."

Hunter identified the disguised voice as the kidnapper's. He held the cell phone up to Tashya's ear and leaned close to her, so both of them could listen.

"I didn't tell you to stop," the kidnapper half demanded, half whined.

So the kidnapper was either watching them or having them watched by someone reporting back to him.

"I practice safe cell. I don't drive and talk on the phone."

"Get going."

"Where?"

"Ditch the tails, and I'll be in touch."

After the dial tone blared in their ears, Tashya looked at the blinking tracer and turned up the radio. "Did you get his location?"

"He didn't stay on the line long enough."

Hunter now had several choices. He could pull a quick U-turn, chase down his tails and confront them. Or he could lose them. Either option was risky. Both had advantages and disadvantages. However, he also had to consider the princess's safety and weigh the danger to her against how much he might learn from questioning his tails.

Tashya reached over and placed her hand on his. "What are you thinking?"

"I'm weighing your safety against Dimitri's and Nikita's," he told her honestly.

She squeezed his hand tight enough to dig her nails into his flesh. "Let's get something straight. The kids have to come first."

"I'm not sure if confronting those tails will gain us any information—but it will put you in jeopardy."

"What would you do if you were alone?" she asked, her tone impatient.

"I'm *not* alone."

"You didn't answer my question."

"I'd go after the tails. Force them to tell me who they work for."

"There's your answer," she insisted.

It wasn't that simple. However, Hunter knew she was right. But placing her in danger went against the grain. "I could drop you off here—come back for you afterward."

"And maybe they'd grab me while I was alone." She spoke calmly. "I'm safer with you. Even if you drive us straight into danger. So get on with it."

The cell phone rang. Expecting the kidnapper, Hunter turned off the radio and put on the speaker option, so Tashya could listen.

"This is Officer Nefi, Highness. We questioned those degenerates separately. They all gave up the same story. They were paid in cash by a guy on the street who goes by the name Georgi Petrov. They described him as a stocky man in his mid-fifties with black hair and dark eyes, who speaks English with a Bulgarian or Hungarian accent. All three men claimed that they had no idea that they'd been hired to attack Your Highness. They were told you were a businessman who'd cheated a merchant and needed to be taught a lesson."

"How far was that lesson intended to go?"

"These criminals aren't stupid, Highness. They aren't going to admit to attempted murder."

"What about Georgi Petrov?" Hunter asked. "Have you any records on him?"

"Sorry, Highness. We believe the name is an alias."

''Thank you, Officer. If anything else turns up, please inform me immediately.''

He clicked off the phone, and Tashya's tone was somber. ''We don't have anything to go on. Whoever is doing this knows how to hide themselves.''

''We'll just have to be smarter.''

''How?''

Hunter turned the radio up. ''First, we ditch this car.''

She reached for the phone. ''I'll have Nicholas arrange for another car to—''

''No. It's too easy to tap into the palace phone system. If Nicholas arranges transportation for us, the kidnapper may find out.''

''We can't buy a car at this time of night. Even the cab companies are closed.''

''We're going to steal one.''

Chapter Seven

Steal? Hunter wanted her to steal a car? The thought bothered Tashya on several different levels. Stealing was wrong. She didn't believe in taking some hard-working citizen's car just because she didn't have one of her own. A car was an expensive item; it took many hours to earn the money to buy one. She imagined the upset owner, the inconvenience and anger at the loss, the time lost from work to report the stolen vehicle to the police.

Hunter wanted her to steal.

Tashya had been brought up by her father with a strong sense of justice and duty to her people. She held her position to serve Vashmira's citizens, not to take from them.

And he wanted her to steal.

She couldn't even justify stealing a car for the greater good. It wasn't as if she was fighting a war for her people. Stealing a car served only her purpose, her convenience. It was wrong.

But so was kidnapping and possibly murder. Weren't the lives of two little boys worth more than a car? Was she simply wrestling with her conscience so she could justify an illegal action?

Hunter glanced at her. "If it makes you feel any better, when we return, you can have the palace write the owner a check."

She quieted her conscience by telling herself she would do whatever was necessary for Nikita's and Dimitri's safety. Really, she didn't have much choice—not if she wanted to live with herself.

Of course, there were no guarantees they would live through the night. Hunter stepped on the gas, and she braced her hands on the seat and door, her heart surging with fear. She stared straight ahead, not daring to look at the speedometer, not even daring to say a word of protest. Losing those tails had to be done and speeding was their only option right now.

Hunter zigzagged through the city streets, changing lanes to steer around wide corners. Several minutes later they left the city behind and entered a residential neighborhood. "Hold on, Princess. We're almost there."

"Where?" From the maps he'd studied, he must know exactly where he was going, but she'd never been in this section before and didn't recognize the area.

He turned a corner and slammed on the brake. The car slid to a stop by the river. He parked in the middle of a boat ramp. "Grab your bag and get out."

She did as he asked, stepping into the night air and feeling vulnerable without the armored plating around her. Hunter took his duffel from the back seat and tossed it into the grass. "Wait here."

He got back behind the wheel, rolled down the windows and bent below the dash. She had no idea what he was doing. Then the car headed straight for the water. She gasped.

At the last moment Hunter opened the door and rolled out of the car as easily as Dimitri tumbled from bed. Hunter swiftly shoved to his feet to watch the car roar down the ramp and splash into the water. The heavy armored vehicle sank beneath the surface and out of sight with one giant sucking gurgle.

"We're hiding our tracks?" she asked.

He nodded. "Now we need a new set of wheels."

They strolled across the street where expensive homes overlooked the river. They walked past several vehicles before Hunter stopped beside a dark Mercedes coup that looked sleek and powerful.

Kneeling, he placed his duffel on the ground and pulled out a thick ring of keys.

She'd expected him to pick the lock. Talk about being prepared. He walked around carrying sets of master keys; she wondered how many cars he'd stolen.

Judging by his efficiency and the two seconds it took him to find the correct key, he'd stolen quite a few. Two minutes later, in their stolen vehicle, he drove them back the way they'd come at a much more sedate pace. She turned off the air conditioner and tried not to feel guilty for settling comfortably into the plush leather seat. At least he'd stolen from a household that could probably afford to lose their car and undoubtedly had insurance.

"Are we going back to find the tails?" she asked him, glad she was free to speak in a normal tone and without a radio blasting.

"They're gone."

"Since when?"

"Since I mentioned going after them."

She leaned back and closed her eyes. "If the armored car was bugged, do you think they know that you aren't my brother?'' she asked, opening her eyes and watching as he turned onto a highway that led toward the airport and the mountains beyond.

''We'll know soon enough. If the kidnapper calls back, it's probably safe to assume he still believes that I'm the prince.''

And if he didn't call…she might never see Dimitri and Nikita again. The horrible thought brought tears to her eyes. She wiped the tear off her cheek with the back of her hand. ''How long…'' She stopped herself. Hunter couldn't possibly know when the kidnapper would call again. Pestering him with useless questions would only distract him from…from what? She had no idea where he was taking her next.

He checked his rearview mirror every fifteen seconds like clockwork. ''My guess is that it's going to be hours until we get that phone call.''

''Hours?''

''The kidnapper's plan to take us out at the phone booth failed. I don't think he had an alternate strategy.''

''Is that good or bad?''

''Although he kidnapped the boys out of the palace quite efficiently, it means we're probably not dealing with a professional. Let's just hope he tries again and doesn't panic.''

She swallowed her frustration. She wanted the phone to ring now. She wanted to get this over with. ''So what do we do while we wait?''

''We sleep.''

Romance wasn't exactly high on her list of priorities at the moment and she wasn't sure what she thought about sleeping arrangements.

He turned into a parking lot outside Vashmira's main airport. "We should rest so we can be fresh," he said. He parked in the long-term parking lot amid the Eurocar rentals where she imagined it might not be noticed for several days.

"Come on, Princess. I need to steal another car and then we can find a bed for the rest of the night."

"WAS STEALING ANOTHER car really necessary?" Tashya asked Hunter after she settled into the discrete white sedan.

"Probably not necessary, but I like to take the safest option." As he drove past a well-lit area, he glanced over at her. Dark circles under her eyes weren't from shadows but from stress and fatigue. Although Hunter never once forgot that she was a civilian on a dangerous mission for which she'd received no training, he'd failed to consider how the strain of knowing the kidnapped children so well would affect her. He'd met Dimitri and Nikita just once, but they were her brothers.

After one meeting the two boys had reminded him of puppies, curious and lovable. However they had grown up around Tashya. She'd probably held them in her arms since they were babies, watched their first steps, heard them speak their first words. The danger they might be in had to be much harder for her to bear than for him—a relative stranger.

Working under that kind of stress tended to wear trained agents down. For Tashya, it had to be pure hell.

He wished he could give her something else to think about and considered allowing her to take part in some of the decisions. While he had no intention of abdicating his responsibility for this mission, if he could treat her more like a partner, she might feel as though she had a little more control over the outcome.

"Where do you think we should hole up for a few hours?" he asked her.

"I suppose the five-star Vashmiran Crown Hotel is out of the question?"

"It would be better to go somewhere more discrete. Somewhere we won't be recognized, if that's possible."

"There are some special license hotels that are near the historic attractions in the old neighborhoods."

She directed him to a pretty street of pastel-painted old wooden houses, rebuilt and refurnished like period pieces. Tashya put on sunglasses and knotted a scarf over her hair, a temporary disguise that often worked. She secured a suite at the hotel while Hunter hid his face behind a newspaper. She paid in cash, and then they were taken to their rooms by a sleepy bellboy who informed them that the restaurant opened at 7:00 a.m., the bathhouse an hour later and that the café across the street served Turkish coffee and baklava or *asure*—pudding made with nuts, cereal and raisins—for breakfast.

Hunter tipped the bellboy, then set Tashya's backpack in the bedroom. He made sure the drapes were closed and the windows locked before he went back into the living area. "Go ahead and take the bedroom, Princess. I'll sleep on the couch."

She looked from his six-foot frame back to the five-foot couch. "It's too little for you."

Now was no time for her to turn considerate. Even discussing the sleeping arrangements had him on edge. "Have you forgotten I can sleep anywhere, even sitting upright in a chair? I'll be fine."

She hesitated again outside the door to her room. "You'll wake me if the phone rings?"

"If you like."

Something in his tone must have clued her in that he had no intention of waking her up until he felt it was necessary. She frowned at him. "If we share the bed, I'll hear the phone ring, too."

No way would he be able to sleep if they shared a bed. No damn way. Just imagining her next to him— her soft breath rising and falling, her skin close enough to take in her sweet scent—would lead his thoughts down a path he'd decided he could never take. Yet he had no intention of telling her how she affected him. Kissing her had been a mistake that he couldn't make worse by going even further—like sleeping in the same bed.

"Go on." Hoping the gesture appeared light-hearted, he waved for her to move along and leave him. "I have a few things to do."

Yeah, like twiddle his thumbs. Like pace in frustration. Like think how good it would be to have accepted her invitation.

She stepped into the bedroom, and he could no longer see her, but that didn't mean he couldn't envision her getting ready for bed. He doubted she'd had room in that backpack for a nightgown. He wondered if she slept in the nude, and his mouth went dry at the thought. She'd probably sleep in a T-shirt, a cuddly soft shirt that would outline every curve, caress every hollow.

When he heard her turn on the water in the shower, Hunter knew better than to attempt a combat nap. He wasn't exhausted enough to turn off his mind. How could he sleep when he imagined her standing under the shower, water coursing through her hair, over her face, raining between her breasts?

He slammed his right fist into his left palm, hoping the sting in his palm would remind him that he had work to do. From his duffel, he pulled out a laptop computer and uplinked to a satellite. He entered three eighteen-letter/number combination passwords and downloaded a top-secret encryption program.

He searched a military database that wasn't supposed to exist but which the U.S. intelligence community used to identify hostiles, terrorists or spies. He entered the name ''Georgi Petrov'' and waited for the computer to sift through thousands of names from hundreds of countries.

The computer told him no matches had been found. Hunter wasn't surprised. He'd assumed the name had been an alias right from the start. Next, he withdrew the wallets of his three assailants. One by one, he entered their names into the database. Again, no matches were found, and Hunter assumed they were simply low-level thugs who had never drawn the interest of any international network.

Hunter withdrew from the U.S. database and drummed his fingers on the table. Should he request a crack from U.S. intelligence to break into the Russian, Bulgarian or Turkish Web sites to search for the names? Hunter possessed the security clearance to request that high-level kind of search, but he knew every search left a trail, and this early in his investigation, he couldn't justify the risk.

Hunter shut down his computer and repacked the equipment. Unfolding a map of the immediate area, he studied it carefully before he took out the tracing device and checked it. The first two digits of the phone number had been identified. He matched them to a phone book directory to make sure his memory was correct. It was. The kidnapper's call had come from somewhere inside Vashmira's interior. From the mountain region. If they didn't receive a call by morning, he intended to start driving in that direction.

"Hunter?"

Tashya opened the bedroom door. She walked into the living area wearing a shirt that barely reached her thighs. Her legs, incredibly toned from riding her horses, forced him to keep his gaze anywhere by there. She had marvelous legs, long and lean and…erotic. He lifted his gaze and realized she wasn't wearing a bra, either.

Oh, God.

She was pure temptation.

He raised his eyes to hers, figuring that would be safe. But the need and desire he saw swirling there turned him on even more than her magnificent body.

He almost growled at her. His voice was so curt that it didn't resemble the laid-back Alexander's in the least. "What?"

"I can't sleep."

He had to look somewhere besides her eyes, somewhere other than her breasts, or those sexy legs. He stared at her feet and realized he'd never seen her bare toes before, sinfully polished, gleaming pink toenails that led to the delicate arches of her graceful feet.

Blood surged to his groin. At his loss of control over his body, he turned away from her, stumbled toward the window and stared outside.

He saw nothing in the black pane of glass but her

reflection, feminine, soft and hot. Hot enough to fry his nerve endings with just one searing look. Damn. He couldn't go near her. Not now. Not with his heart pounding with need, lust filling him up from his soles to his scalp and making clear thinking difficult.

"Go back to bed, Princess."

"Come with me."

Come with me. Those words tore into his resolve— *to her bed*—battered his determination.

It took every ounce of willpower he possessed to turn to face her. Her expression was proud, her eyes hopeful and welcoming, her lips soft and inviting. But he couldn't...

"We can't afford any distractions right now."

She spoke softly, her voice curling around him like a blanket. "Is that what I am to you, a distraction?"

"Don't."

She came to him, put her arms around his waist and laid her head against his rapidly beating heart. "I'm worried about the boys, and Sophia and my older brothers. Just hold me. Please, just hold me."

She didn't know what she was asking, didn't understand the conflict raging inside him between needing to protect her and needing to make love to her. Her heat combined with her fresh scent almost undid him. Duty had been drilled into him first by his father, then by the military and then by the CIA. He'd been tempted before during a mission—but never like this. If he waited one second longer to free himself, he'd never find the strength. He yanked backward, out of her arms, retreated a step.

"This isn't going to happen." He folded his arms across his chest, controlled his ragged breaths through sheer strength of will.

At his cold words she flinched, then courageously lifted her chin. "What's the matter?" Boldly she let her eyes drop to the straining bulge in his slacks. "You want me. I want you."

"And what about tomorrow?" He cupped her chin and looked deep into her eyes, knowing he caused her pain but unable to stop himself because he damn sure knew that refusing her was the right thing to do. He might want her, but he cared most about protecting her. He wouldn't go against the code of honor he lived by—not when letting down his guard could cost her life.

She shrugged. "We may be dead tomorrow."

"Look, Princess. I've survived much tougher assignments than this one, and I have no intention of failing. You're going to have a tomorrow, a next week and a next year, so I'm not going to take advantage of your enticing…suggestion."

She tossed her hair over her shoulder. "You aren't taking advantage. I'm offering."

"I'm refusing."

"I could change your mind…but then *I* would be taking advantage of you."

She turned from him, and with the grace of a queen, walked into the bedroom and quietly shut the door.

He bit back a groan, knowing he had hurt her, aching with wanting her. Still he'd done the right thing. So then why did he feel so bad?

TASHYA WANTED TO SHAKE some sense into the man. She was worried sick about her brothers and she couldn't sleep. The waiting, the not knowing if the boys were even alive, made her feel helpless. Princesses weren't supposed to feel helpless, and she was having difficulty dealing with not getting what she wanted. Okay, she was pampered, maybe a little spoiled.

But Hunter was being totally unreasonable. There was no good reason not to spend what was left of the night enjoying one another's company. She wanted his arms around her. She wanted to rest her head against his broad chest and share childhood stories. She wasn't asking for a lifetime commitment, but for a few hours of pleasure so she could forget for a while that she might never tell the boys a bedtime story again. Never bathe them or kiss their sweet little faces.

What better way to get to know Hunter, to learn to trust one another?

But did Super Spy see her point of view? No way. He had to stick to duty and honor and all those noble things.

She supposed she should feel humiliated by his rejection, but how could she after she'd seen the evidence of his desire? Instead, anger at his unilateral decision ruled her emotions. Who gave him the right to assume what was good for them both?

Stubborn fool. She bounced onto the bed, then stared at the ceiling with her fingers laced behind her head. All her life she'd been surrounded by powerful men, men who made life-and-death decisions and who ruled her country and those of their neighbors. Most of them were good men who went into public service out of a need to help their people.

But damn it. She'd never wanted one of them the way she wanted Hunter. Perhaps the danger had lowered her inhibitions, but his protectiveness aroused her.

She reminded herself that Hunter was more a soldier waging an attack than a politician planning a campaign. Still, she was a grown woman who knew exactly whom she wanted—and just because that man was set on doing things his way was no reason for her to give in. She may have lost this battle between them, but she was determined not to lose the war.

When Hunter's cell phone rang, she forgot her anger and rushed out of the bedroom.

He attached his tracing device to his cell phone, pressed the speaker option that allowed her to hear the conversation, then let his phone ring three times before answering. "Yes?"

"Alex, it's Sophia. Have you heard anything?"

Her stepmother sounded distraught, and Tashya's heart hitched. She leaned forward and spoke into the speaker. "We answered a phone call from the kidnapper at the National Museum, but we were attacked. Alex fended the thugs off, and we're expecting the kidnapper to contact us at any time. We really shouldn't tie up this line."

"I understand." Sophia hesitated. "I thought you should know a few things. Neve is nowhere to be found. She's simply disappeared, never made it home. Ira thinks the girl might be working with the kidnapper."

"Have Ira check her bank accounts for any large deposits," Hunter suggested in Alex's voice.

"Stephan—I mean, Major Cheslav checked through military records for me. Records General Vladimir refused to let me see. Neve's father died during the revolution. She comes from a good family.''

"Is there something else?" Alex asked.

"I'm so worried about Dimitri and Nikita. I was going to ask Nicholas to put off the discussion of women's rights in the cabinet until after we find the boys. It's possible that someone took the boys to get Tashya out of the palace in order to counteract the princess's influence with the cabinet.''

"You fear that if the vote comes too soon, then our enemies will have no use for my little brothers?" Hunter asked, following Sophia's logic and filling in the blanks.

Sophia had never agreed with the women's rights legislation that Tashya was trying to have enacted. Sophia believed women should remain at home and that their careers should consist of taking care of their families. Tashya had nothing against Sophia's beliefs, but she thought all women should have the right and the opportunity to choose a career if they wished to have one. Could Sophia be correct? Had this entire kidnapping scheme been concocted by someone who wanted her out of the way while the votes were tabulated?

Or was there another reason altogether? One she couldn't fathom.

"I see no harm in delaying the votes on these issues," Tashya agreed. "Go ahead and speak to Nicholas, but I suggest you wait until morning. After all, he and Ericka are newlyweds on their honeymoon."

Hunter disconnected his phone and carefully examined the tracer device. "Get dressed. Hurry."

By his intensity, she knew something was wrong. Her pulse automatically shifted into high gear. She hurried into her room, but not before Hunter turned out the lights, pulled his weapon, and carefully peeked out the window.

She'd never dressed and packed so fast in her life. Breathless, she returned with her backpack slung over her shoulder to find he'd opened the rear window of the suite that overlooked a lower roof and that he'd already tossed his duffel onto the crumbling shingles.

She didn't ask questions. But she had difficulty climbing through the window with her palms damp with perspiration. Hunter placed a protective hand on her head, and she ducked under the sash and slowly eased onto the roof. Although dawn had yet to arrive, the night sky was brightening, hinting at the daylight to come within minutes. On the rooftop, they were easy targets, and the ground looked sickeningly far away.

Hunter slung the duffel over one shoulder and led Tashya toward the rear of the building. The gentle pitch of the roof made walking relatively easy. She had no fear of accidentally falling. But somehow, they had to drop to the ground.

"Over there," Hunter whispered, then tugged her toward a corner that couldn't be seen from the front entrance.

She followed him, never once doubting that these maneuvers were necessary and that something had alerted him to danger. Hunter wasn't a man who would endanger her or frighten her unnecessarily. She trusted his judgment with her life. If he told her to jump off the three-story-high roof, then she would jump off the roof. She just prayed she didn't freeze up on him out of fear of breaking her neck.

"How are you at tree climbing?" Hunter asked.

She swallowed hard as she gazed at the narrow branch that extended from the tree to the roof. "Tree climbing isn't exactly a mandatory course in exclusive Swiss finishing schools."

"Hand me your pack."

She did as he asked. Then he dropped to his stomach, lowered his duffel and her pack as far as he could reach, then released them. They landed in the grass with a hard thud that made her heart jerk. That could have been her body smacking the ground.

"Someone traced Sophia's call to us. I expect company sometime soon."

Company? Hunter had a way with understatement that jarred her nerve endings.

"Why did you allow the call to last so long?" she asked as she contemplated crawling out onto the branch.

"Because...I want to see who shows up."

Chapter Eight

Hunter had been delighted to see that someone had traced Sophia's call. Since the beginning of his impersonation of Prince Alexander, Hunter had been forced to react instead of taking action and going on the offensive. But now that he knew someone wanted to pinpoint their location, Hunter could take charge. Whoever showed up would have a nasty surprise waiting for them.

However, first he had to get the princess off the roof. The sooner the better. Dawn was only minutes away.

He pointed to their first goal, a thin branch that arched from the roof edge back to a massive trunk. "Are you strong enough to swing arm-over-arm until you reach that lower and thicker branch with your feet?"

"I can try."

She didn't sound confident. He couldn't help admiring her for recognizing her own weaknesses and being brave enough to try to overcome them.

"Okay." He unfurled a rope he'd taken from his duffel. Quickly he fashioned a makeshift harness around her hips and feet. "There's no need to worry—"

"Yeah, right."

"If you fall, I'll catch you."

"Why can't you just lower me to the ground with the rope?" she asked reasonably.

"Because…this rope isn't long enough." A fifteen-foot drop probably wouldn't kill them, but they could easily break bones.

Hunter reached into his pocket and handed her an earpiece with a miniature microphone/receiver. "Place this in your ear. The mike will pick up a whisper, and I'll talk you through it."

Without hesitation, she placed the tiny piece into her right ear. With a deep sigh, she then faced the branch. She would have to lean over the roof edge just to reach the slender handhold, then swing arm-over-arm, a total of maybe four or five times to reach the relative safety of the thick branch with her feet. And she would have to do it quietly.

Hunter couldn't go with her. The thin branch wouldn't hold both their weights. He secured the free end of the rope harness to his belt, then wrapped a firm arm around her waist. "I won't let go until you have your hands set."

"Give me a little push, okay?"

He leaned forward with her as far as he could, but didn't dare push her. "Go for it."

She jumped. Her hands caught the branch. Her feet kicked and the leaves rustled.

"You're doing great. Wait until your feet stop rocking, then let go with one hand and swing forward. Do it fast."

She didn't move. He heard her breathing heavily,

and he wondered if he had misjudged her determination and strength. But wouldn't she have protested if she thought this was beyond her ability? Maybe not. She was one determined lady. He hadn't even bothered to ask if she had a fear of heights. Now certainly was not the time.

"Don't look down, Princess."

"Okay."

She released one hand, swung and regrasped the branch.

"Great. You're doing fine. Don't rest too long."

Hunter unfastened the extra rope from his belt and let out more of the line attached to her harness. If she fell now, he could hold her weight. But if she fell after he let out a few more feet of line, the strength he would need to hold her after the drop would be enormous. There was no chimney to wrap the line around to absorb some of the shock. Carefully, he kneeled and wrapped his end of the line several times around the branch, then secured it back to his belt.

As she kicked and struggled forward, he prayed the branch would not break. "That's good. You're almost there."

He broke into a sweat. Each forward swing of her body looked weaker. On the last swing, she'd barely regrabbed the branch.

Her breathing was ragged, and she grunted. He tensed. "One more time. Take a deep breath. After this one, your feet can find a solid perch, and you can rest."

"I—"

"Don't talk. Use everything you have." If she waited too long, she'd weaken further. "Go."

His voice might have been only a whisper, but he hoped to communicate his urgency.

She swung out and her feet thudded, slipped, then found the solid limb. Slowly she settled, sitting on the thick branch, her back against the tree trunk.

"Hold on tight with both hands, Princess. I'm letting go of this end of the line. I'll reel it in after I get there."

"I'm not going anywhere."

In three quick swings he was beside her. "You okay?"

With an annoyed frown, she sucked on her finger. "I broke a nail."

He almost chuckled in relief. But they didn't have time for levity. They still had to reach the ground. Luckily the tree branches remained close together and provided a natural ladder until the last ten feet. He used the rope to lower her to within three feet of the ground, and then she simply let go of the rope and landed on her feet.

They retrieved their packs without attracting attention, and Hunter skirted the woods, circling back to where he could watch the front entrance without being seen, hiding them behind a thick hedge.

He removed binoculars from his pack and handed them to Tashya. "You're more likely to recognize someone than I am."

The sun's morning rays touched the treetops with a soft golden radiance, and Tashya tipped her head back to catch the light. Her skin, rosy from her exertions, glowed with a luminescence that made his breath catch. With her hair tumbling around her face and a smudge of dirt on her cheek, Tashya looked more like a schoolgirl playing hooky than the reigning princess of Vashmira.

"Sorry you didn't accept my offer?" she asked softly, obviously aware of his admiring glance and not the least bit discomfited by it.

"Sorry" didn't even halfway describe the depth of his feelings. She had no idea how much he'd wanted to throw away his training, forget about the mission and make love to her for the rest of the night. Yet, if he had to make the decision again, he would make the same one. Two people on the run had no business making love to one another. Especially when one of them was responsible for the other's safety. He couldn't let her distract him from the danger—no matter how delectably tempting her offer.

And she had been oh, so deliciously tempting. Even now, he had to fight against leaning forward to smooth the smudge from her cheek and inhaling her sweet scent. Instead he faced the entrance, peered at empty asphalt and hoped that when the enemy showed, she would recognize him.

TASHYA DIDN'T KNOW where her boldness in pursuing Hunter had come from—except maybe fear and desperation. Last night, the idea of making love to him, clinging to his strength, had seemed the right thing, the only thing in the world that would heal her at that moment. When she'd turned to him she hadn't thought with her head but had let her female instincts lead her into temptation.

She'd discovered and tapped into a deep well of emotions that she hadn't known she had. Fear for her family that had caused her to turn to Hunter. Feelings of need and lust and wanting to give as much as she wanted to take had wrapped her in a whirlpool of self-discovery.

But last night after he'd refused her, the wellspring of emotions had run dry, leaving her with a hollow emptiness. She hadn't slept, tossing and turning, worrying over the boys, hoping they would see the kidnapping as an adventure and not be scarred from their experience.

Last night she'd been angry that Hunter hadn't wanted to help her forget her fears. This morning she felt weary but stronger knowing that he'd refused because he was a man of integrity and honor. The same protective spirit that made her want to lean on him also made him strong enough to put aside his own desires for the sake of his mission.

Hunter might deny his attraction to her with a warrior's tenacity, but like the waves of water lapping against rock, she would eventually wear him down. So she could afford to be patient. Yet, the waiting wouldn't be easy. She could choose to use the gifts nature had given every woman to go after the man she wanted. She had lived at court long enough to understand the art of flirtation, long glances into one another's eyes, an "accidental" touch, a flip of her hair over her shoulder—yet she didn't want to incite just his lust.

She wanted more.

Hunter pointed down the road. "Car's coming."

Tashya focused the binoculars and her thoughts on their current predicament. As she shifted her concentration from the personal to finding her brothers and the danger they faced, she realized that she was adapting. Shifting her thoughts with a speed that amazed her.

She didn't recognize the light gray vehicle. "The driver's too far away for me to make out her features."

"Her?"

"Definitely a her. She has long black hair." Tashya lowered the binoculars in disappointment.

"Look again," Hunter urged. "Maybe it's Sophia."

"If you think Sophia would kidnap her own children and then pretend to all of us that she's upset, you don't know her very well."

"Uh-huh." He didn't believe her.

"Sophia is practically a saint. She doesn't plot. She doesn't even like politics."

"Just look again to be sure, okay?"

Tashya sighed, raised the glasses and gasped.

"What?"

"It's Neve. Dimitri's and Nikita's nanny."

"Let me see." Hunter reached for the binoculars, and she handed them over to him. He widened the lenses to fit his broader face, then stared through them. "She's probably working with the kidnapper."

"Or maybe Sophia sent her," Tashya suggested.

Hunter shook his head. "Sophia doesn't know our location—not unless she traced her own call to us and is responsible for kidnapping the boys."

Tashya couldn't believe that the woman who had so loved her father, the woman who had acted as her mother, the woman who didn't appear to have one ambitious bone in her body, could coldly use her own children to cause Alex and Tashya harm. "Someone else could have traced Sophia's call. Maybe the chief of security or General Vladimir or his aide, Stephan Cheslav."

"Or maybe the nanny has concocted this scheme with the help of one of them," Hunter conceded. "We'll know soon enough."

"Are we going to follow her?"

"*I'm* going to question her." He took his weapon off safety and jammed it into his jacket pocket as Neve parked the car. "Stay here. If there're people hidden in that car, I don't want you in the line of fire."

She didn't like his order, but she understood. "By the way, Alex sometimes calls her Little Neve and always speaks to her as if she's part of the royal family."

"Got it."

Hunter rubbed the dark stubble on his chin. "You should be able to hear our entire conversation through the earpiece. If anything happens...if I can't return—" he handed her the car key "—don't call anyone. Just drive straight back to the palace."

"I understand," she told him. Whether she would do as he said depended totally on the circumstances. That he was about to leave her, even for just a few minutes, had her nerves on edge, but outwardly she was determined to remain calm. "Go on. I'll be fine."

She didn't need him distracted with worry over her. Without another word, he moved silently and quickly out of their hiding spot behind a thick hedge.

"Be careful," she whispered.

"Careful is my middle name," he whispered back through the microphone/receiver hidden in his ear.

She expected him to head straight for Neve, who walked through the front entrance. Instead he acted as if he was taking a morning stroll. One hand in his pocket, the other free, he ambled along a sidewalk, watched goldfish swim in a pond, and finally checked out Neve's car.

"No one's hiding in the back," he told her.

Although she appreciated the communication between them, she couldn't squash her fear. Hunter could be walking into a trap. Another car could roar down the drive, a car filled with men carrying guns. It was possible, although unlikely, that while they had been climbing out onto the roof and down the tree, men had entered their suite. Perhaps someone had recognized the prince and princess shortly after they'd checked in and had called the palace.

As possibilities drifted through her thoughts, she fought to steady herself. Hunter knew what he was doing. He sensed danger the way a horse smelled fire. If he barreled into trouble, he could handle himself. She'd seen him fight expertly with only his bare hands as weapons, had seen his familiarity with a gun and had no doubt he was an expert shot. Nor would he take Neve's seeming innocence for granted.

Yet how could Tashya not worry? Checking her watch, she realized that only two minutes had gone by. Not even long enough for Neve to reach their suite. Certainly not long enough for Hunter to have caught up with her.

Tashya ached to ask Hunter where he was and what was happening. However the man needed to concentrate without interruption. So she bit her top lip and fretted and waited, each moment achingly, impossibly long.

She picked up faint background sounds. The rattle of a newspaper, the ding of an elevator. Luggage wheels rolling across the floor. The rattle of dishes.

It almost sounded as if he had gone into the dining room.

Damn him. Why didn't he say something? Anything.

HUNTER HAD LEARNED that when he impersonated Prince Alexander, he couldn't sneak anywhere. Someone always recognized the prince of Vashmira. He would have preferred to ditch his disguise and follow Neve in secret. But instead, he hid behind another newspaper and his sunglasses and waited for her to come out.

While he waited for her to join him on the veranda, Hunter watched to see if anyone followed her. He saw no one. When she exited the hotel lobby, he stepped from his concealed spot in the shadows. When she recognized him, she broke into a dead run, threw her arms around him and burst into tears. He patted her back and led her down the sidewalk toward the spot where he'd left Tashya waiting.

He wanted the women together where he could be close enough to protect Tashya if she needed him. He also wanted the princess's take on whatever Neve had to say. Tashya knew the nanny and she would be the best judge of the woman's veracity.

"I'm so glad I found you, Highness." Neve wiped the tears from her eyes with the backs of her hands. When he pulled her toward the hedge, she hesitated, slightly wary, slightly alarmed. "Where are we going, Highness?"

"Someplace private where we can talk."

He urged her along, not about to take no for an answer. If she tried to scream, he was prepared to cover her mouth with one hand and to use force to drag her behind the hedge. But she came willingly.

When Neve spied Tashya, she sobbed even harder. The princess put her arms around the boys' nanny and hugged her. "Everything's going to be all right, Neve."

"No, it isn't." Neve sobbed. "If the boys come to any harm, I'll never forgive myself."

Hunter handed the crying nanny a handkerchief and restrained his impatience, realizing that she needed to calm down before she could tell them a coherent story. "Can you start at the beginning and tell us what happened?"

"I helped kidnap the boys." Her slender shoulders shook. Her nose turned red, and she sniffled into the handkerchief.

Tashya frowned. "You? Kidnapped the boys?"

"Someone broke into my house, and they beat my mother. She's in intensive care at the hospital." She shuddered then continued. "I got a note. The note said that if I spoke to no one, they wouldn't kill her. I was so scared. I thought about telling the security chief, but I was afraid to use the phone. I wanted to give him the note, but I could never get him alone."

"So what did you do?" Tashya asked.

"I tucked the boys into bed like always. I was supposed to leave the suite door unlocked."

"Did you?" Hunter asked.

"I still hadn't decided whether or not to cooperate," she told them, clearly miserable. "When I walked out the door, someone grabbed me from behind and placed a rag over my nose and mouth."

"Did you see who grabbed you?" Hunter asked.

She shook her head. "I smelled something sweet

and went to sleep. When I woke up, I was with Dimitri and Nikita, locked in a shed with a dirt floor.''

"Where?" Tashya asked.

"In the mountains. I think I can take you there," Neve offered.

"Not so fast." Hunter stopped her, unwilling to make one move until he'd carefully considered every facet of her entire story—the details of which he had yet to hear. "You said you were locked in a shed?"

"Yes."

"How did you get out?"

"A guard brought food. I flirted with him, and then hit him over the head with a rock." Tears started to flow again. "God. I may have killed a man."

She sank to her knees in the grass, dropped her head into her hands and sobbed. "He was young. Just a kid in the military."

"He wore a uniform?"

"Yes. He seemed so young to be a soldier. I may have...ended his..." She hiccuped.

Tashya placed an arm around her shoulders and smoothed back her hair, trying to comfort her. "The boys weren't hurt?"

"They were still sleeping. I couldn't wake them. I think they were drugged. I couldn't carry both of them. If I left one alone, the other would have awakened alone and been terrified. You know how much they like to be together."

"I know."

"So I figured I should run for help."

"Then what happened?" Hunter asked, highly suspicious that this little slip of a girl had managed to escape. It was much more likely that she was working with the kidnappers, planning to lead Tashya and him into a trap than that she was telling the truth.

"I rushed out the door. There was a car out back with keys in it."

How convenient, Hunter thought.

Neve kept talking. "I took the car and drove toward the boys."

"Toward the boys?" Hunter asked.

"I intended to carry the boys to the car and take them with me. But a second guard was bending over the man I hit with the rock, so I...left."

"Then what happened?" Tashya asked.

"I had no idea where I was. There were mountains and no houses. I took the only road. I think a car chased me, but I'm not sure. I got away. I tried to find a town to call Sophia, but I was lost."

Hunter controlled his impatience. Either Neve had been through an ordeal or she was a very good actress. But parts of the story didn't add up—such as how had she found them?

"I kept driving east and south. I don't know the mountain area, didn't even know which direction to head. I'd overheard the guards talking about where you were and hoped you might be close. When I stopped to ask for directions and discovered you were only an hour away, I came here. Should I have called the palace? Or the police?"

"You did fine." Hunter kneeled in the grass beside the tiny nanny. "Do you think you can find that cabin again?"

"It was dark. I was so scared. I think I can, but I'm not positive," she told them.

Earlier she'd offered to take them to the boys. Now she seemed unsure that she could find her way. Had she made a mistake when she'd sounded so sure that she could find the cabin? Had she realized he was suspicious and had then changed her story hoping he might forget her earlier offer?

If she was telling the truth, she'd had an incredible string of luck. Escaping from a locked room and her guards. The keys conveniently left in the car. Finding them after conveniently overhearing the guards. Or had Sophia traced their call and told Neve where to find them?

Was Neve working with Sophia? Were the children really in danger? It was possible that Hunter and Tashya were risking their lives for no reason. If Sophia had kidnapped her own children, she certainly wouldn't hurt them.

But it was just as likely that Sophia was innocent and the chief of security or the general had traced the call. That a soldier was guarding the boys could mean the military was behind this entire incident. General Vladimir had been loyal to Nicholas's father, but was he as loyal to the new king?

What of the general's aide, Stephan Cheslav? Had he gotten close to Sophia so he could kidnap her children? Could he be allied with Sophia or the nanny? But what would be his motive?

Hunter sorted through the multitude of possibilities, knowing he didn't have enough information to form a valid conclusion. But right now they had only one lead that might take them to the missing children, and that lead was sobbing her eyes out.

Hunter picked up the binoculars and focused them on the road. The bright early morning sunlight revealed that no one else had shown up.

No one had shown up that he could see, he corrected himself.

There could be a roadblock or an ambush just waiting for them to make a move out of here. While they had no choice but to try to find the children, he still had a few tricks up his sleeve.

Chapter Nine

Tashya was learning to read Hunter. Although his expression never changed and he hadn't relaxed one muscle as he'd listened to Neve's story, she sensed that he was skeptical of the nanny's innocence. Tashya supposed in a career like his, trusting anyone always put someone else's life at stake. Tashya didn't blame him for remaining wary when she, too, had doubts. Neve's story had stretched credibility. Although Tashya had trouble believing that anyone in the court's inner circle would resort to kidnapping and murder, *someone* at the palace had to be behind the children's disappearance.

"Ready to head out?" Hunter asked Neve, whose sobs had quieted, and Tashya, who wondered if going on alone with just the three of them was best.

"Wouldn't the search go faster if we called in help?" Tashya asked.

Hunter shook his head. "You mean, like the military or the police? Have you forgotten that Neve said the men holding the boys wore military uniforms? And a police search would be impossible to keep quiet. The kidnapper would get wind of our intentions and certainly move the boys to another location."

Maybe kill them. Tashya helped Neve from the grass to her feet. "You still think the boys's best chance is us?"

"The sooner we leave, the sooner we can find them." Hunter hurried them toward the parking lot. He didn't head toward either the car they'd driven last night or the vehicle Neve had appropriated.

Instead, with his master set of keys, he unlocked a late-model blue sports car with a narrow rear seat. Quiet and pale after her emotional telling of her story, Neve slipped into the back without a word, apparently unaware the "Prince" was stealing a car. Tashya settled into the front passenger seat while Hunter placed his duffel in the trunk.

He slid into the driver's seat, tense and wary. But he drove at the speed limit. "Our phone call with Sophia was traced. Whoever traced the call will probably be here shortly."

Neve frowned at Hunter. "How do you know?"

"Because if I was a bad guy, that's what I'd do. I'm hoping if we leave now, we can avoid an attack."

If Neve thought it strange that the prince of Vashmira was an expert tactician, she didn't say so. Alex had had military training, so perhaps Hunter's actions weren't that suspicious.

"If you hide in the back seat, I could drive," Tashya suggested somewhat tentatively. "The kidnappers won't be looking for two women."

"If you weren't so recognizable, that might be a good suggestion." Hunter swerved around a bend in the road and relief washed through Tashya. She'd felt obligated to make the offer, but she really wasn't qualified to drive. Under normal circumstances she could manage through streets that didn't have much traffic, but she wouldn't have been able to keep the car on a highway at this speed, never mind a two-lane country road. She vowed that if she got out of this alive, she would practice her driving. She didn't like being dependent, hadn't realized how much she relied on other people, like her driver, until recently.

Hunter seemed so sure that someone was coming for them. Her stomach tightened into a hard knot of anxiety. They were no longer in an armored car. Her normal security guards weren't there to protect her. She didn't even have so much as a butter knife with which to defend herself.

She suddenly realized that she very much wanted to live. She wanted to watch Dimitri, Nikita and the baby grow to manhood. She wanted to hold the children Nicholas and Ericka would someday have. She wanted to watch Alex fall in love. She wanted to help guide her country through the new millennium, to ensure the passage of new laws to protect their women. She wanted to fall in love, have children and grandchildren. She wanted to travel. She wanted to get to know Hunter better, much better.

Fear seemed to have sharpened the clarity of her thoughts and her senses. In the bright sunlight, their car was such an easy target. A bullet could penetrate the windshield in the blink of an eye, and she would never know what happened. One moment she would be alive. The next she would be gone.

Get a grip.

She couldn't allow her runaway thoughts to panic her. She had to have faith in Hunter's abilities. He certainly handled the car with the skill of a race car driver. Even when forced to veer from the pavement to the rock-strewn shoulder to avoid a darting squirrel,

Hunter kept the car under control, and last night he'd assured her that he'd lived through much more dangerous missions.

Tashya began to feel calmer and was even beginning to think that all of Hunter's precautions were for nothing. There had been no reason to climb across the roof and down the tree. No reason to steal a vehicle. At the sight of clear road ahead, she started to relax.

"Oh, God," Neve shouted from the back seat, and pointed, her hand shaking.

Two cars up ahead waited on either side of the road. As Hunter drove by, the cars pulled onto the road behind them, following them. Tinted windows lowered and gun muzzles pointed in their direction. Several shots pinged off the back window, shattering the glass.

"Get down," Hunter ordered.

He no longer drove straight ahead. He swerved from side to side, no doubt trying to throw off their pursuers's aims.

Tashya flung herself sideways. Her head ended up resting on Hunter's leg, her cheek pressed to his thigh. She clung to the seat, cringing as more shots pinged off the car.

Their car suddenly skidded. Hunter swore, fighting to keep them from going sideways. "Damn. They blew out a tire."

The tire shredded on the pavement, leaving the stench of burned rubber. Worse, their vehicle bounced and jarred them so badly that she bit her tongue. Only her seat belt prevented her from falling to the floor.

Hunter didn't release his foot from the gas pedal, but the engine coughed. Tashya lifted her head slightly, but all she could see were trees flashing by, their branches like tentacles sucking at the car, scraping the paint.

Hunter had driven off the road.

"Ladies, when we stop, get out of the car and run. I'll stay behind and cover you."

"I smell gasoline," Neve shouted from the back seat.

"They probably hit the gas tank. Don't worry, the car won't explode like in the movies," Hunter assured them.

As the car slid into a clearing, Tashya unstrapped her seat belt. Through the shattered back window, she saw no sign of their pursuers in the trees behind them. She grabbed her backpack. They'd probably have only seconds to run and hide in the dense brush once the car finally stopped sliding on the damp grass and loose dirt.

Hunter jammed on the brake. Finally the car halted. Hunter yanked out his gun, popped the trunk and reached for his duffel.

"Go. Go. Go."

Heart leaping up her throat, Tashya dashed after Neve into the woods. Stickers clung to her socks and branches whipped her face, but she kept sprinting. She breathed in huge gasps, not so much from exertion but from fear—and not for herself so much as for the man who had stayed behind.

She glanced back over her shoulder to see one car filled with their pursuers enter the clearing. Hunter swung his arm as if he were pitching a baseball. A second later the car exploded.

He must have thrown a grenade.

She couldn't see the second car, but she heard the engine roaring as if the driver was determined to run

Hunter over. Moments later shots from automatic weapons sliced the air with a savagery that seemed to shake the ground.

What seemed like hours but was probably only half a minute after the initial shots, the gunfire behind them lessened in intensity. Neve collapsed, her face red, her breath coming in huge pants, and Tashya didn't urge her to go on. They were far enough from the battle to be safe—if Hunter had taken out the occupants of the second car. If he'd failed, all the running in the world would do them no good.

Tashya longed to go back to Hunter's side to try to help him. Leaving him alone to face the enemy while she and Neve ran away seemed the ultimate act of cowardice. She desperately wanted to return and fight. Yet her presence would distract Hunter. If he stopped to worry about her, he could make a mistake and get killed.

The overpowering scent of burned flesh infiltrated the wooded area, settling around them like a pall of gloom. Tashya wished she could see what was happening, but smoke blocked her view. Suddenly the gunfire ceased.

Neve grabbed her hand. "Come on. We should keep going."

Tashya yanked her to a halt. "I'm not leaving."

"Highness, your brother told us to—"

"I don't care what he said. He could be injured." Tashya hadn't wanted to disturb Hunter's fighting mindset. She understood well how important sharply focused concentration was. When she jumped her horses in competitions, she never even noticed the crowds who watched. She never heard the announcer, blocking everything out except her rhythm and the stride of her horse beneath her. So she understood the necessity of not disturbing Hunter during his fighting mode, but with the cessation of shooting, the battle appeared to be over.

With the outcome unclear, Hunter might need help, and she wasn't about to go off and leave him. She released Neve, and cautiously started to retrace their mad flight. "You go on if you want."

Tashya didn't wait to see what the nanny would decide. After the ear-splitting gunfire, the silence had her nerves on edge, her ears straining to pick up clues as to who might still be out there. Something had to be wrong, or surely Hunter would have caught up to them by now.

Although determined, Tashya was careful. She used the natural cover of the dense woods to keep her hidden. She tried to walk silently and to avoid stepping on branches that could crack beneath her feet. She found herself holding her breath, listening for the slightest sound. There was nothing. Not a bird, a frog or a cricket.

Neve came up beside her and whispered, "It's creepy. Maybe we should head for the road and flag down a car, or call the police."

Tashya shook her head. "Alex thinks that the kidnappers are listening to the police radios. We need to be careful." Stooping, she picked up a stout branch. Tentatively she swung it through the air to test how long it would take to connect and how much force she might need to use.

Neve tugged Tashya's sleeve. "Did you hear that?"

"What?"

The hair on the back of Tashya's neck stood on

end. An object in the trees appeared much too straight to be part of nature. She squinted and decided she was looking at the barrel of a gun.

Where was the shooter? Hidden behind the trunk of an oak?

Tashya picked up a rock and tossed it toward the gun. Nothing moved.

Now what?

Maybe the direct approach wasn't such a good idea. Circling around might take longer, but be smarter and safer. No way could she become lost. The stench of the burning car would lead her to the clearing.

"This way."

Tashya hurried to her right, arbitrarily picking a direction. If they angled toward the battle scene and emerged from a new direction, perhaps they might figure out what had happened to Hunter before anyone else spotted them. From there, she'd have to wing it, depending on what she found.

She prayed Hunter was still alive, but had to thrust her worry from her mind. Instead she focused on hiding herself, edging forward slowly, making as little noise as possible. Next to her, Neve copied her movements.

Tashya had no idea how much time had passed or how far they'd run. The journey back seemed to take forever. Despite the shade from the trees, the morning sun beat down on her head. Perspiration broke out on her forehead, and she yearned for a cool shower.

Neve stepped on the back of Tashya's shoe. "Sorry, Highness."

"Can we dispense with my title?" Tashya pulled

her shoe back on, accidentally hooking her broken nail. Pain shot up her hand.

She raised her hand toward her mouth, intending to suck on her bleeding finger when a man stepped out from behind a tree. Forgetting her bloody finger, she gripped the branch and started to swing.

It was Hunter. Alive and looking very unprincely. His clothes were dark with soot and possibly blood, and also torn in several places. His hair had lost its I'm-the-most-desirable-bachelor-in-the-country look, and the gleam in his eye was anything but fraternal. Even Neve seemed to be eyeing him strangely.

Tashya retracted the swinging branch awkwardly and tried to deflect any doubts Neve might be suddenly having about the prince's identity. "Alex, I've never seen you so rumpled in your life."

Hunter paid no attention to the threat of her branch, instead, he stared at the blood trickling down her hand and hurried to her.

"Are you okay?" Tashya and Hunter both asked one another at the same time.

Neve nervously giggled.

Hunter frowned and reached for Tashya's wrist. "You're bleeding."

"I told you I broke a nail."

"You didn't tell me you ripped half of it off." He slung the duffel from his shoulder, reached inside and pulled out a first-aid kit.

Neve looked from Hunter toward the burning car. "Are we safe? What happened to those men that were chasing us?"

"They won't bother anyone ever again." Hunter opened the kit, took out a bottle of alcohol and uncapped the top. "This is going to sting." He poured the clear liquid over her wound.

"Ouch." Tashya tried to jerk her hand back.

Hunter held her still, his fingers a manacle around her wrist. "Sorry. Almost done."

But he wasn't almost done. He'd found a tube of antiseptic and squeezed ointment onto her raw nail. Then he wrapped her finger in gauze. "The ointment has a numbing agent in it and the bandage should help protect you from reopening the wound."

Tashya pulled her hand away from his the moment he finished his ministrations. "Thanks."

The sudden sound of a helicopter's whirring rotors overhead had Hunter urging them under the canopy of a thick shade tree where they wouldn't be spotted. She suspected that the chopper was simply delivering supplies to a nearby town and its occupants had no idea of the death and horrible destruction in the woods. But Hunter wouldn't take any unnecessary chances. When it came to survival, Tashya trusted Hunter's judgment and didn't even try to guess what he'd do next.

Hunter looked from Tashya to Neve. "If the cops find the tracks we left driving off the road, they'll search the woods and find our pursuers's cars and their bodies. They'll block the road and seal the obvious exits. Maybe bring in dogs to track us."

Neve looked at him skeptically. "Highness, can't you call in the military to get us out of here?"

"I could—if I was sure that General Vladimir or his aide wasn't behind my little brothers's kidnapping."

Tashya couldn't help agreeing with the nanny's obvious doubts. "It seems as if the military is going to extraordinary lengths just to keep women out of their ranks.''

Neve gasped. ''You think that's why they took the boys? To keep you quiet during the voting?''

Tashya's views were well known among the educated palace women. While not all of them openly agreed with her, many had offered private encouragements.

Hunter shouldered his duffel. ''Right now, we need to set a false trail. Are you both up for a little hike?''

''How little?'' Tashya asked. Still, she picked up her backpack and followed Hunter. ''May I remind you that we have no food or water?''

''My military training included survival courses,'' Hunter offered.

''It did?'' Neve muttered under her breath.

Tashya said nothing more. While Hunter knew how to survive in the woods, Alex didn't. While Neve didn't say another word, she clearly had doubts. Tashya supposed if the nanny guessed that Hunter was impersonating Alex, it wouldn't be so bad—as long as she wasn't in league with the kidnappers. But if she was part of the group, and she was suspicious of Alex, wouldn't she keep those doubts to herself?

This circular spy logic made her head ache. As Hunter led them away from the road and the burning cars and the dead men, Tashya wondered about their chances of success. They'd started in an armored car, traded it for a stolen one and were now reduced to walking. Yet, on the positive side, Neve believed she could find Dimitri and Nikita. Tashya hoped the police wouldn't find the cars they'd left behind until tomorrow. At least she couldn't yet hear dogs barking on their trail.

Hunter led them in one direction for a hour. Then he made them walk through a creek. Several times they left the creek only to backtrack again. "We're laying a false trail for dogs and trackers."

"You sure you haven't been watching too many Western movies?" Tashya asked.

"They use this ploy often because it works." Hunter led them back downstream and over a rocky area before heading in a new direction. "There's another road that parallels the one we came in on. We'll head out of the woods there."

They'd left the creek hours ago, and Tashya tried to think positively, but as the hours wore on without either food or water, her spirits began to sink. She didn't dare ask Hunter if he knew where they were— fearing his answer. Instead she concentrated on Hunter's back, placing one foot in front of one the other, taking just one more step.

That's what her life consisted of now—taking just one more step. Then another.

HUNTER PRESSED the women harder than he would have liked. However, if the bullet-strewn cars and bodies behind them were found, he expected an extensive investigation to be launched immediately. He'd searched the pockets of the men he'd killed and had learned very little. He suspected that their cars were stolen, their weapons bought on the black market. None of the men had carried identification. So these were professionals—not particularly well trained, but one step up the ladder from the thugs he'd left in police custody.

He didn't waste time thinking that he would have preferred to take one alive to question him. He cut his losses and moved on. Although his stomach rumbled with hunger, finding water was much more important. Under ideal conditions, a human body could fend off starvation for upward of two months by living off its tissues, but it could not last nearly as long without water.

Finding water was one problem. Making sure it was fit for human consumption was another. Luckily, he had chemical purification tablets in his duffel.

He'd hoped to cross the woods before nightfall or to come across a deserted cabin with a working well, but he had seen no signs of civilization since they'd left the road, no water since they'd abandoned the creek earlier in the day. Hunter had no doubt he could keep the women alive in these woods, but the nanny was already suspicions of him. The more skills he exhibited, the more suspicious she would become. However, he wouldn't let them go to sleep thirsty tonight.

Hunter knew that water tended to be found near the bases of hills and that game trails often led to water holes. He'd been following a deer trail for the past two hours. Finally it paid off with what he'd been looking for: a creek tumbling down from the hills.

"Water." Neve licked her lips. "You found us water." She hurried to the creek bank and scooped up a handful.

"Don't drink it." Hunter opened his duffel and found his water purification tablets and his canteen. He handed the items to Tashya. "Fill the canteen. Add two tablets and wait a full ten minutes to make sure they dissolve before you drink."

He pulled several other items from his duffel. "You both rest, and I'll try to find us some dinner."

He could read a thousand questions in Tashya's eyes. But she didn't ask them, no doubt unwilling to risk increasing Neve's suspicions. He placed a sealed container of matches in her hand. "After you rest, why don't you build a fire?"

Tashya frowned at him. "You plan to be gone long?"

"I'll be back as soon as I can."

Clearly she didn't feel comfortable in the woods. However, Hunter felt safer in the wild than he had at any time since he'd entered the country. With the false trails he had laid, he was reasonably sure they wouldn't be found for hours. Out here, the most dangerous animal they might come across was a bear, and if it attacked, his weapons would protect them. In the palace, recognizing one's enemies wasn't so easy. Neither was dispensing with them.

So he welcomed the respite from danger, even if it would only last for a short while. He didn't think it would rain. There was no reason they couldn't eat a meal and catch a few hours' sleep.

Ever since he'd seen Tashya's bloody hand, he'd promised himself to take better care of her. When he was afraid a stray bullet had nicked her, the moisture in his mouth had disappeared. When she'd told him that her injury was the broken nail that he'd paid no attention to earlier, he'd winced with guilt. He'd just assumed a manicure would fix her problem. He hadn't taken the time to find out that she had an extremely painful injury. If the finger became infected due to his careless assumption, he would only have himself to blame. Instead she'd suffered in silence, a trait he hadn't expected from a pampered princess.

But then Tashya had many unprincess-like characteristics. Too many of them quite attractive. Luckily, pretending to be her brother forced him to keep his growing feelings under strict control. With the nanny along, he could not afford even a warm glance in Tashya's direction. With Neve in the picture, their hours together in the woods would be fraternal, although his thoughts were anything but.

Reminding himself that the women were probably as hungry as he was, Hunter stopped his walk through the woods, removed his knife from its sheath and attacked the bark of a birch tree. The inner bark was sweet and sustaining, and could be eaten raw. After collecting a sufficient amount, he added pine needles to his pockets to make tea, found several pine nuts the squirrels had missed, pigweed for greens, and for dessert, a few handfuls of elderberries. Unfamiliar with the local variety of mushrooms, he left those alone since many could be poisonous.

He returned to their camp pleased with his find. But his satisfaction quickly turned to concern at the sight that awaited him.

Surrounded by stones, unlit firewood, which was stacked neatly in a circle, awaited a match.

The women were gone.

Chapter Ten

Hunter searched the ground carefully for signs of a struggle. He saw nothing to indicate that the women had been overpowered. Likely they'd gone off into the bushes to answer nature's call. Still, he hesitated to call out. If they had been taken, he didn't want to warn their captors of his presence.

Normally composed under pressure, he didn't like the way fear surged through him, urging him to rush, to fight, to find his woman—especially when he needed to think. He couldn't afford to go off half-cocked in the wrong direction. He couldn't afford to let his concern overpower his critical thinking. He couldn't afford to make a wrong move.

Giving himself a few moments to settle down, he wrapped the foodstuffs in a spare shirt from his duffel, then rested it against a tree, knowing he'd move more quickly without having to carry the extra bulk. Intending to scout a wide circle around their makeshift camp, he estimated that he hadn't been gone more than half an hour. With everyone on foot, they couldn't be more than two to three miles away.

But if he guessed wrong and chose the wrong direction, he might never find them. He could lose hours if he didn't pick up their trail right away.

About to begin a large circle around the camp to attempt to pick up their tracks, he heard the sound of women's laughter. The happy sound had come from upstream, and the tense muscles in his chest immediately eased. Tashya and Neve were probably taking advantage of the combination of water and privacy to bathe.

His relief caused him to sag with his back against a tree. He forced himself to breathe deeply. He silently cursed himself for worrying for no reason. But once the worry for their safety dissipated, other emotions rose to take its place.

The vision of Tashya naked under the dappled light of the trees, water splashing over her perfect skin, her hair slicked back and water droplets glistening on her eyelashes held him rooted to the spot. Blood rushed to his groin. He clenched and unclenched his fingers in frustration, banishing the enticing image. He should check on the women, but he was no Peeping Tom. A few more giggles assured him of their safety.

He set about lighting the fire and preparing supper, doing his best to ignore the flaming heat in his groin. Normally he had better control over himself. But, normally, he worked alone. He didn't eat and sleep and converse twenty-four hours a day with a woman. He didn't listen to her bathe. He certainly didn't think of her as belonging to him when he well knew they couldn't be together.

Tashya and Neve returned refreshed and happy to see him. He felt grungy by comparison and intended to wash up later. Out of sorts with himself and his unruly reactions, needing to protect the princess and to deal with his own longing to make love to her, he sat downwind of both women and tried not to look at Tashya with anything except brotherly affection.

Neve sat cross-legged by the fire. "Didn't you say something about dinner, Highness?"

Hunter handed her a piece of birch bark. "We don't have a pot or pan. But if you gnaw on the bark, you'll find the meat sweet."

Neve hesitated. Tashya had no such compunctions. She bit at his offering with enthusiasm, her bright white teeth flashing as she nibbled.

At the taste, Tashya's eyes lit up. "This is quite good. Perhaps we could have the palace chef add it to our regular menu."

Hunter handed over the greens and nuts to them, then stuffed his canteen with pine needles. "We can have hot tea."

Tashya leaned over to look at his supplies. "And berries. Alex, I never knew you could be so resourceful."

"Our father insisted that I know how to do more than order a meal in a gourmet restaurant. Actually, Nicholas was much more enthusiastic about camping than I was. Although I have to admit, I never thought any of Father's lessons would prove so useful." He gave Neve his best sheepish smile. "If Lady Madeline could see me now, she'd probably run for the hills."

"Oh, I dare say, the lady would be willing to share anything with you," Tashya teased.

Although Hunter knew she was pretending to the kind of easy banter she shared with her brother, he wished they could again be alone and share a genuine conversation where dissembling wasn't necessary.

With his doubts over Neve's loyalty, they had to take care about every word they spoke.

He used a stick to hang the canteen over the fire. "We'll sleep here."

"And tomorrow?" Tashya asked, apparently not picking up that he only intended to give them a few hours' rest.

"Neve will take us to the boys. The sooner we find them, the less traumatic it will be for them."

Tashya's face paled with worry, and he could have kicked himself for reminding her of the danger they were facing. The princess was often so strong, he forgot how unaccustomed she was to danger.

Neve seemed to notice her upset. The nanny placed a comforting hand on Tashya's shoulder. "I don't think the boys will be frightened. The guards didn't seem the kind to take pleasure in scaring little children."

If Hunter had been the kidnapper, he would have moved the boys immediately after Neve's escape. However, if only lackeys remained at the cabin, they might not report Neve's escape to their boss right away in order to avoid reprisals. Time could be of the essence. Although the urge to charge forward rushed through him, he could only push the women so much.

Hunter needed an excuse to speak with Tashya alone. He took advantage of the opportunity when Neve ambled down to the creek to wash the berry juice from her face.

Hunter pressed a gun into Tashya's hand. "Take this. Don't let Neve know you have it."

"Okay." She shoved it into her backpack and waited for him to explain.

"I need to scout ahead. I'll be gone for less than an hour. Can you stay awake until I get back?"

"Yes."

"Will you miss me?" he teased, and wondered where the words came from. It wasn't like him to be lighthearted during a mission. His little sister always told him some woman would knock the seriousness right out of him, and he'd told her she was out of her mind. She'd only smiled knowingly at him and said something about the strongest men always had the farthest to fall. Was he falling for Tashya? He couldn't recall the exact moment when he'd started thinking of her as his, and it disturbed him that the decision hadn't been made consciously.

"Come back soon." Tashya didn't answer his question.

Neve had returned, interrupting their conversation. "You're leaving?"

"Not for long. I suggest you both get some sleep," he said for Neve's benefit. "We'll leave soon after I get back."

"Why can't we all go together?" Neve asked.

"You need to rest and if I scout ahead, I can take the most direct route through the forest." And check for danger.

Already Neve's eyes were heavy with sleep. She rolled up her jacket and stuffed it under her head. Minutes later she appeared to be sleeping like a hibernating bear.

Still, Hunter kept his voice down, whispering into Tashya's ear. "Don't wake her unless it's an emergency."

"I'll be fine," Tashya told him.

"I don't like leaving you alone with her. But we

have no choice. I won't lead you straight into danger.'' Hunter kissed her lightly on the forehead and then he walked away. Leaving Tashya behind was one of the hardest things he'd ever done—especially when he sensed danger closing in from all directions.

HUNTER HAD RETURNED without finding anything suspicious ahead, and they'd all slept until 5:00 a.m. Tashya and Hunter exchanged several whispered words before she awakened the nanny. Neve seemed a little groggy, but she'd walked steadily through the forest until they'd all arrived at the road that ran parallel to the one they'd left behind them. To the right lay a large town, to the left, a small village.

Hunter left them, entered the small village and returned with a vehicle. Alert as ever, Hunter drove inland toward Vashmira's mountainous region.

He'd obviously taken time to clean up before rejoining them, Tashya though, but his hair still looked as if he'd run his fingers through it to comb it. Had he somehow failed to pack a comb or brush in that duffel of his? Obviously he hadn't forgotten a razor. His chin, minus the dark stubble, looked determined as ever.

Neve's presence had put Hunter and Tashya's more private conversations on hold, and Hunter had done his best to appear no more or less than her brother, yet Tashya could feel an unresolved sexual tension simmering between them. Although their time together had been short and she didn't know the details of Hunter's life, she had come to appreciate his honor and integrity, traits that reminded her of her father and of Nicholas. But she recognized that the emotional strengths—toughness, detachment—that made

Hunter good at his job, were also weaknesses that prevented him from establishing deep relationships. Just as she told herself there could be no future between them, that although she'd rejected the Toad, she would no doubt make a political marriage and that he could make no marriage at all, she couldn't stop her natural inclination to want to respond to him.

She couldn't help wondering what it would have been like if he'd accepted her offer back at the hotel. Would she have been even more reluctant to let him go when his mission was over?

She still wanted to know. Her personal plans might have been put on hold due to Neve's presence and worry over her brothers, but Tashya fully intended to convince Hunter to make love with her. Sooner or later, she would get another opportunity and she intended to make the most of it.

An hour after they left the woods behind in the car Hunter had snatched and the cigarette lighter had partially recharged his cell phone battery, Hunter stopped at a café. They fortified themselves with a hearty breakfast of eggs, baked cheese pastries with blueberry jam and Turkish coffee. Hunter paid in small bills and left a generous tip. Tashya couldn't be sure if anyone in the tiny café had recognized Vashmira's prince and princess. Even with their creekside baths, clean hair and skin, they didn't look like royalty. Their casual clothes showed signs of wear and tear, and her shoes were grass-stained.

Back in the car, Hunter handed Neve a map. "How much farther?"

Neve bit her bottom lip. "I'm not sure." With a sigh of frustration she laid the map across her knees and peered out the window.

Hunter and Tashya exchanged a long look. Neve had fled in the dark. Obviously she'd been terrified and hadn't paid too much attention to her route. They could be on a wild-goose chase, but since the kidnapper hadn't called them, they had no other leads to go on.

They drove past mountain hostels that catered to tourists whose idea of a vacation was a long hike into the hills, before entering the small town of Sarnokov. The charming houses of wood and stone had steeply pitched roofs, colorful assortments of flowers in their window boxes and neatly trimmed lawns. Just a few blocks long, the town of Sarnokov had formerly been a mining town and now relied on manufacturing rugs for tourists. Prosperity could be seen in the late-model vehicles on the streets, children riding new bicycles on the sidewalks and the modern fire station.

Neve's voice rose in excitement. "This town looks familiar. There should be a one-lane dirt road up ahead with a cow sign over a tavern."

For the first time since breakfast, Tashya's hopes rose. Although Hunter had told her that even if they found the cabin the kidnapper might have moved the children, maybe they could find a lead. A clue left behind in haste.

She couldn't help worrying over Dimitri and Nikita. What would they think when they woke up in unfamiliar surroundings? As smart as Dimitri was, he would realize the danger he and Niki were in. She prayed he wouldn't try anything foolish. A fresh sense of urgency washed through her. They had to find the boys soon.

"There's the cow." Neve pointed to the sign over the tavern. "It's not far now. Maybe a mile or two."

Hunter stopped the car. Before Tashya could ask him why, he explained. "I'm going in on foot. Alone."

His statement alarmed Tashya. "You may need our help. You can't carry Dimitri and Nikita and fight your way out, too."

"I'm not placing you in danger." His voice was hard as granite.

"Have you forgotten the kidnapper has demanded that we exchange ourselves for the boys? You need me to go with you."

But what about Neve? Tashya could almost read Hunter's doubts. The prince and princess could turn themselves over to the kidnappers in exchange for releasing the boys to Neve, only to find out that Neve was in on the kidnapping and their efforts were all for nothing.

Tashya had no wish to throw her life away. If she had to die, she wanted it to mean that her little brothers would live. Yet what choice did they have but to trust Neve, especially since Hunter refused to phone for additional help?

"I know you're suspicious of my escape," Neve interrupted. "But I swear I'll do my best to make sure the boys get back to the palace safely."

"I don't doubt your heart is in the right place," Hunter told the nanny, reminding Tashya how well and easily he could lie. "But the kidnappers may not hold up their end of the agreement. They could come after you. If someone manages to kill me, Tashya, Dimitri and Nikita, that would leave only our older brother and Sophia's baby in line for the throne."

Tashya stared at him in surprise. "You think someone is trying to wipe out our entire family?"

"It's a possibility." Hunter took out his weapon and checked the clip. "Our father was assassinated last year. Just weeks ago, a murder attempt on Nicholas and Ericka failed. With American Secret Service agents protecting the king and queen, they are relatively safe for the time being. So our culprit may be targeting the more vulnerable members of our family first, then intending to go after Nicholas when security around him relaxes."

The more Hunter spoke about the dangers to her entire family, the more Tashya's patience wore thin. This was her family they were talking about. Hunter's analysis was all very interesting, but she wanted to go after her little brothers. She wanted to hold them in her arms and to know they were safe. "Surely, there's someone we can call for help? Someone that you trust."

"The only person who has nothing to gain by our deaths is Nicholas."

"So call him," Tashya urged.

"You're forgetting that the palace phone line is probably tapped by the kidnapper. And if we ask Nicholas to join us, I have no doubt he would put his life in jeopardy to try to save our little brothers. The danger of our entire family being wiped out—except for Sophia's baby—is just too great."

Tashya realized Hunter's logic was making sense. His ability to guess at the kidnapper's possible motivation both awed and frightened her. She'd originally believed that the kidnapper might have been trying to stop her work for women's rights, but that had been a self-centered idea. Her politics simply weren't that important. However, if someone wanted to murder her entire family, they could take over Vashmira.

Neve's voice shook with either fear or excitement. "So then it's just the three of us?"

"Looks like it," Hunter agreed, albeit reluctantly. His dark expression hadn't changed, and at the moment, his grim mouth looked nothing like Alexander's.

Tashya's pulse had skipped when Hunter had changed his mind about leaving them behind. He might issue orders like a general, but that he'd willingly compromised meant that he respected her opinion—something she hadn't expected from an obvious loner like him.

Nevertheless, she exited the vehicle with trepidation. Since Hunter had never requested that she return the weapon he'd given her last night, she clutched the handle and fingered the trigger under the cover of her jacket pocket. Whether she was ready to shoot if necessary was another question.

By now she knew Hunter's tactics well enough to realize he wouldn't walk along the road, where he would give up the element of surprise and make an easy target. While the phone call may have alerted the kidnapper to their destination and they might be expecting someone to arrive, they couldn't guess when.

After hiding the car behind a dilapidated barn, Tashya and Neve followed Hunter deeper into the woods. He chose a path that paralleled the road. The hike proved arduous because it was an uphill climb and there was no natural animal trail to follow. None of them spoke, saving their breath for the task ahead.

Hunter set a brisk pace, walking so silently that Tashya felt like an elephant trampling every crisp leaf. Forced to knock aside branches to avoid having them strike her face, she winced with every crackling sound.

Neve brought up the rear, and Tashya wondered if the nanny was herding them into danger. Had she been an innocent, her mother threatened as she'd claimed?

With every step, Tashya's nerves stretched tauter until her muscles ached. Surely they had to arrive at the cabin soon?

Just when she'd resigned herself that the hike would never end, Hunter stopped, raised his fingers to his lips and pointed through the trees. The structure appeared more shed than cabin. There were no windows in the tin walls. The roof was flat, and she saw no signs of life. No people. Not even a parked vehicle. No electric or phone lines were attached from poles to the structure, which appeared very temporary. She'd bet the royal jewels that whoever owned this acreage had no idea the illegal hideout existed.

Hunter raised a pair of binoculars to his eyes and took a good five minutes to look over ever detail. Tashya used the opportunity to rest against a tree trunk, and Neve did the same. Tashya would have given anything to know what the nanny was thinking. Had she really escaped from the kidnappers? Or was she part of their plan?

IT WAS QUIET enough to hear a finch flutter through the trees. Quiet enough to hear bees buzz around the wildflowers. Quiet enough to hear mosquitoes hum hungrily around the bare skin of Hunter's face, neck and wrists. But he remained still, careful to keep the sunshine from reflecting off the binocular's lenses and back toward the hut, which didn't have windows but might very well have peepholes.

He wished he had time to observe for several hours before he considered the next step. But the children would be frightened, possibly hungry, definitely in danger. The sooner he could find them, release them and return them to Sophia, the better.

The hut sat in the middle of the clearing. From the raw dirt around the perimeter it was clear that the structure hadn't been there long enough for grass and weeds to grow. Yet, whoever had built it had carefully considered the location. First and foremost, it was isolated. He doubted the sound of a gunshot would reach town. Dead bodies here might not be discovered for days, weeks, even months.

Hunter didn't like leaving Tashya alone with Neve while he checked out the cabin. But what choice did he have except to trust in Tashya's ability to use the gun if the nanny turned on her? Not one to dwell on the limits of the options open to him, he placed the binoculars back into his duffel.

As if sensing that he'd come to a decision, Tashya shoved to her feet and approached him. He plucked a leaf from her hair and twirled the stem between his fingers. She raised her eyes to his, and for a moment, he had to fight the urge to swoop down and let his lips claim hers. He would have stopped fighting if Neve hadn't been watching.

Instead, leaning toward her, he spoke softly into her ear, close enough to inhale her scent and tuck it into his memories to savor later. "Wait here. I'm going in."

"Okay." She agreed without hesitation, but he thought he saw a flicker of annoyance in her eyes.

When he looked again, her expression appeared normal.

However, he wasn't totally surprised that when he darted into the clearing and toward the shed, she dashed right behind him. His heart kicked into his throat at the danger she'd placed herself in. In the bright sunlight, out in the open, he knew better than to send her back. Once they reached the hut wall, she'd be safer than if she tried to recross the clearing.

Damn her. She'd agreed to stay behind without the slightest hesitation, and then she'd done exactly what she pleased. Stubborn woman.

He flattened himself against the wall, every sense on alert. His keen sense of smell didn't pick up the scent of unwashed bodies, or even a whiff of shaving cream, cologne or toothpaste. He heard no human noises. No talking, no whispers, no sounds of hurrying feet. Without a window to peek through, he headed straight for the back door.

Hunching low, he reached for the doorknob. It was unlocked. The door swung open of its own accord.

Hunter didn't move a muscle. Beside him, Tashya held perfectly still. Again he strained his hearing, sniffed the air, and closed his eyes to a near squint so his pupils would adjust before he rushed into the dark hut.

He glanced inside cautiously, and a filament of fiber stretching across the lower part of the doorway caught his eye. A trip wire?

He pointed to it, and Tashya nodded. However he couldn't be certain she understood the significance of tripping the wire, so he took a chance and whispered, "If you trip the wire, the entire building could explode. Stay here, Princess."

"Okay."

"I mean it."

"Okay."

In case someone waited inside ready to shoot him, Hunter wanted to go in fast and hard. But if there was one trip wire, there could be others. He would have liked to spray the building with bullets. His firepower could easily penetrate the aluminum walls. But suppose the boys were inside? He couldn't risk using a weapon.

Hunter could think of no way to minimize the risk of going through the doorway. So he just stepped carefully over the trip wire and hoped for the best.

It took a moment for his eyes to adjust to the darkness. Food wrappers, empty drink cans and the assorted trash of a hideout littered the hut. However, there was no furniture, no garbage cans, not even a cubbyhole where the boys could be.

It was empty.

Chapter Eleven

After seeing that there was no one in the shed, Hunter focused on the booby-trapped doorway. The simply constructed trip wire could have been devised for a variety of reasons. To take out the prince and princess when they arrived. Or to cover up the crime scene. Or both.

He shone his flashlight on the wire, following it back to the fuse, igniter and firing device that he immediately recognized as a Russian-manufactured Spitblaster 23-7. Set off by a prearranged frequency. A sound could detonate the explosion. Any sound— like an airplane flying overhead. A scream. A gunshot. Was that why Neve had waited outside? Was she about to issue the sound that would set off an explosion?

Tashya stepped inside. Did the woman never listen to orders? Without hesitation, Hunter raised a finger to his lips, signaling Tashya to silence. He grabbed her hand, made sure she stepped over the trip wire and yanked her out the door. They both stumbled outside into the bright daylight. Neve was nowhere in sight.

Hunter's phone rang.

"Run. Go. Go. Go."

Hand in hand, they made it five steps before the blast behind them tossed both of them into the air. Hunter hit the ground hard, rolled, at the same time searching for Tashya.

She shouldn't have followed him.

He ignored the flaming pieces of metal raining around them. He ignored numerous cuts and bruises. He ignored the heat and smoke. He had to get to her. She had to be okay.

This was his fault. As he crawled to where she lay on her side, unmoving, fear grabbed his gut. She faced away from him, silent and still. In the heat of the flames, he couldn't take time to check her breathing. Grabbing her up into his arms, he lifted her, carried her away from the smoke and gently laid her down at the edge of the forest.

Her face was pale beneath the grime. A cut on her forehead bled freely. All his years of training had come down to one stupid decision. He should have sent her back.

About to perform CPR, he leaned close. When she opened her beautiful blue eyes, clouded with confusion, and stared into his, relief eradicated some of his fear.

She coughed, then took a deep breath but didn't try to move. "What happened?"

"My cell phone ringer triggered an explosion."

"Explosion?" She turned her head and looked at the flaming hulk of a hut. "We were in there?" She sat up, her eyes growing wide with terror. "The boys…"

"Weren't there," he assured her.

"Thank God."

"You weren't supposed to be there, either." He frowned at her. "I told you to stay back but—"

"I didn't listen," she finished. "I remember following you inside." She frowned. "Then it all gets kind of hazy."

"Short-term memory loss is common with a concussion. Let's hope that's all you suffered." He examined her limbs and torso, but saw no sign of injury. "Are you hurt?"

"My finger." She held up the dirty bandage that protected her broken nail. "But I already did that, right?"

"Yes. Lie still for a few minutes. It's normal to feel dazed after an explosion."

"*You* seem fine."

He stood to fetch his duffel bag and withdrew his canteen. "I have a hard head."

"No kidding."

He unscrewed the cap, lifted her head and held the canteen to her lips. "Small sips."

She swallowed several times then pushed the canteen toward him. He took several deep gulps, letting the cool water wash away the smoke and fear he'd swallowed.

Tashya peered around the clearing. "Where's Neve?"

"I haven't seen her since we entered the hut."

"Maybe she ran for help after the explosion," Tashya suggested.

"Maybe." Or maybe she'd taken the opportunity to flee back to the kidnappers. Or had she simply remained behind in the woods because the prince had given her an order?

Hunter's phone rang again.

He didn't immediately answer it. "It's probably the kidnapper calling to find out if we survived the explosion."

The phone kept ringing.

Tashya clutched his wrist. "If they think we are dead they may not have a reason to keep Dimitri and Nikita alive. Answer it."

Her thinking had quickly cleared. Her resolve to save her little brothers hadn't wavered.

The phone rang a third time.

Hunter hesitated, testing her determination. "The boys may not still be alive."

"Answer the damn phone," Tashya demanded.

Hunter did as she asked. "Hello."

"It took you long enough." The kidnapper's distorted voice conveyed anger.

Hunter used Alex's voice to make his demand. "We're going back to the palace right now unless I speak to Dimitri and Nikita."

"No."

Hunter clicked off the phone.

Tashya rose to her feet, her eyes furious. "What did you just do?"

"They'll call back," Hunter told her, hoping he'd made the correct decision.

"Suppose they don't? Suppose they never call again? Suppose we never see Nikita and…"

Hunter tried to gather her into his arms, but she planted her palms on his chest and pushed backward, clearly still furious with him. "You have no right to make unilateral life-and-death decisions."

"Yes I do."

"It's my family."

"And this is my job. I'm very good at it, so let me do what I do best. Okay, Princess?"

Before she could answer, the phone rang again. Hunter raised an eyebrow. He waited until it rang a third time before he replied. "Dimitri?"

"I'll put him on," the kidnapper agreed.

Hunter heard several clicks, as if the call was being relayed, which made him think that the kidnapper on the phone was in a different location from where the boys were being held.

"Uncle Alex?"

"Are you and your brother hurt?"

"We want to go home."

"Can you take care of Nikita and be brave just a little longer?"

"Yes, sir."

Hunter's heart went out to the five-year-old, who seemed to be holding up remarkably well. He hadn't been crying. He hadn't sounded hysterical.

Hunter expected the kidnapper to make an immediate demand. But the line went dead.

"What happened?" Tashya asked him.

"I suspect the kidnappers are having communication difficulties."

Tashya's face looked hopeful despite the tears brimming in her eyes. "How did the boys sound?"

"Alive."

At his response, Tashya burst into tears. Not tiny delicate tears, but giant tears that made her eyes go red. Without a second thought he gathered her into his arms, smoothed back her hair and simply lent her his shoulder to cry on.

He said nothing. Just held her and rocked her gently, knowing she needed to release the pent-up stress. The disappointment of not finding the boys, the explosion, then Neve's mysterious disappearance were simply too much for her to endure.

So he held her, giving her the opportunity to react like an ordinary woman under huge pressures instead of as a princess who never felt free to show her emotions. He'd occasionally comforted his sisters, and tears didn't unnerve him the way they did some men.

However, holding Tashya so closely was causing his body to react in inappropriate ways. In another moment she would have to notice his erection, and he tried to pull away, but she clutched him so tightly that he couldn't separate his hips from hers.

She sniffled. "I'm...s-sorry."

"It's okay."

"I can't...seem to stop crying and...I'm making a mess of your shirt."

"It's okay."

"I must look a mess." She sniffled again. Then stiffened, obviously realizing how she'd affected him.

He expected her to pull back. She didn't. She simply wrapped her arms around him and snuggled her head under his chin and against his chest. While he realized Neve could pop out of the woods and into the clearing at any time, the nanny wouldn't think it too odd to see the prince cradling his sister while she cried.

However, if Neve returned and noticed the swelling of part of his lower anatomy, she might have second thoughts about Alex's identity. But Hunter didn't have the heart to pull away while he could give Tashya comfort. The princess had been so brave, waiting until the immediate danger had passed before bursting into tears. He knew his statement that the boys were alive had been merely the catalyst for the release of her restrained emotions.

Hunter wished he could take away her pain, and with his wish came the realization that he'd fallen in love with Princess Tashya.

He loved her.

He should have seen it coming when he'd started thinking of her as his woman. He should have known how he felt when he'd had so much difficulty fighting his own intense reactions to her. Other women and other missions paled in comparison to this one. Tashya was special. Unique. Complicated. He should have known that fighting against wanting her wouldn't have been so difficult if he hadn't been battling the strongest of emotions.

He loved her.

That was why his pulse went bonkers and his thoughts raced uncontrollably whenever she placed herself in danger. That was why he couldn't keep his mind squarely on his mission.

He loved her.

And as he held her crying in his arms, he experienced a tenderness he'd never known before. What the hell was he going to do with these feelings? Feelings that seemed to deepen with every moment he spent with her.

Why couldn't he just lust after her body? Why couldn't he think of her as a career woman who would enjoy a fling? Why couldn't he just take her to bed, make wild, wonderful love and leave the princess and her country behind as a pleasant memory? Why did he have to go and fall for a woman he could never have?

Taking civilians with him on his missions wasn't

an option, and once he finished in Vashmira and moved on to the Cobra assignment, he couldn't even phone or write a letter. For the safety of both of them, he'd have to cut all contact between them. He knew the rules, understood the game, and never before had it bothered him.

He almost groaned out loud. He'd fallen in love with a real live princess who might not be alive much longer if he didn't pull himself together. He was on a dangerous mission, he repeated to himself like a litany. Lives were at stake. Not just his and hers, but her little brothers, too.

He had to stay focused. In one sense, his head had never felt so clear. Admitting his feelings cleared up a lot of his confusing reactions. At least he now understood why his pants were tight enough to make him grit his teeth from the ache. For once, he was glad Alex wore no underclothes. More restrictions might have cut off his circulation.

Hunter knew he could find release and make Tashya forget her troubles for a while. Perhaps they both deserved a little pleasure after all they'd been through. But Hunter was no longer the man he'd been before coming to Vashmira. He could no longer live for the moment with no thought for tomorrow, not with the feelings he harbored for her. Tashya was not the kind of woman he could make love to and then say thanks for the memories. She deserved better.

Hell, he deserved better.

He tried to pull back, but she refused to release him. He spoke gently and firmly. "Let me go, Princess."

She sniffled, stepped back and nodded. But she

didn't look at him. "You have any tissues in that duffel bag?"

He left her and retrieved a piece of gauze from the first-aid kit. "Best I could do."

She blew her nose noisily into the gauze, wiped away her tears with the back of her hand and slumped to the ground. "Sorry about that."

"About what?"

"Crying all over you. I don't know what got into me. I'm not usually so…"

"Human?" he teased.

She still refused to look at him. "I swore to myself that the next time that I flung myself at you, I'd be irresistible. Not a crybaby with a runny nose."

Her self-disgust made him smile. "Maybe I'm attracted to runny-nosed princesses with weepy eyes."

"Well—" she considered the bulge in his crotch without any embarrassment "—you're certainly attracted to something about me. Or is it just that you haven't been with a woman in a long time?"

Her frankness gave him the opening he needed to tell her his feelings, but now was not the time. They'd already been here too long—although he doubted the kidnappers would immediately try for a second hit. Their enemy didn't seem too sophisticated, which was a good thing with the way Tashya kept him half distracted.

He didn't answer her question, just held out his hand. "We need to find Neve."

DESPITE TASHYA'S SPATE of tears or maybe because of them, her mind seemed sharper than usual. She fully realized that Hunter hadn't responded to her question about his sexual needs. Sometimes he could be uncommunicative. But then she recalled how he'd held her so gently, rocking her in his arms while she'd sobbed, and she realized there were hidden depths to the man that strangers would never see.

During the days and nights they'd spent together, he'd rarely spoken about himself. She knew nothing about his life, his family, or his work, but she suspected that he must work for one of the U.S. intelligence agencies. Of course, he could be a mercenary for hire—but his code of honor seemed too strict for that. He'd shared so little of himself, and yet she felt she knew the important things about him. He was dedicated to his mission and capable of intense, single-minded effort, capable of putting his life on the line for her or for children he barely knew. He believed everything must be done "right" and his strong moral code wouldn't allow him to deviate from his chosen path. She didn't know what that path was, but it probably shut out all possibility of any meaningful future together.

Tashya certainly hadn't burst into tears on purpose, yet she didn't regret her moments of weakness—not when her lapse had brought her back into Hunter's arms. Physically, he'd wanted her. His body had told her so, and she was pleased. She just wished he hadn't had the strength to pull away.

She needed some of that strength, needed to believe they would find her little brothers alive and unhurt. Needed his strength to believe the threats to her family would end.

Of course, now was neither the time nor the place for a dalliance. Although Neve was not around to interrupt their privacy, once again Tashya had to put her own wishes on hold. Going out to a pub with friends, then strolling through a park—just a simple date where a couple could exchange information about themselves—had never been an option for her. And maybe it never would be.

However, despite Hunter's reluctance to make love, she was determined to learn whether he had real feelings for her. She knew her thoughts always centered around him. Half conscious from the bomb's blast, her first concern upon opening her eyes had been for his and the children's safety.

He'd repacked his duffel, dusted off her backpack and offered it to her. She stood and slung one strap over her shoulder, prepared to follow wherever he led, whether it be back to examine the site of the explosion, to their car, or further into the woods to look for Neve.

"We need to break the cycle," Hunter told her.

She frowned. "What cycle?"

"The kidnapper phones us and we come running—right into a trap. First the phone booth at the National Museum, then the cabin. We have to be smarter."

"Okay. What do you think we should do?"

He circled the area, obviously looking for signs of Neve while he spoke. "We have several options. We could go public with the boys's kidnapping and offer a reward leading to their safe return."

"I don't think the kidnapper is after money."

"Neither do I. However, I believe the men in military uniforms who have your brothers are merely taking orders. They may not even realize they're doing something wrong."

"What do you mean?"

"Suppose they're honest soldiers who have been

told by their superior to protect the boys from a terrorist attack?''

''You think they'd realize they'd been duped and come forward for a reward?''

''It's possible. We could inform the press, radio, television, newspapers. Millions of your citizens would be encouraged to report suspicious activity.''

''But?''

''The danger is that the kidnapper might panic and…''

''Kill them to avoid being caught?'' She asked the question, knowing the awful possibility had to be considered.

''I've also considered bringing in more help from the States.''

''I'm slowing you down, aren't I?''

''With more help, we could have a crack team of investigators monitoring the phone lines, mail, running down leads. But the more people we bring in, the higher the probability of leaks.''

She sighed in frustration. ''Which will put the boys in even more danger.''

''Exactly.'' He paused and looked over his shoulder. ''You're rather good at considering all the angles.''

She grimaced. ''Life at court is always full of intrigue. It's just usually not so dangerous. How long have you been working…for whoever it is that you work for?''

''Sorry, that's classified.''

She tried again. ''So tell me why you got into this line of work.''

''It's—''

"Classified." She finished for him. "Isn't there anything you can tell me about yourself?"

He remained silent for so long she didn't think he was going to say anything. Finally he asked her, "Does it matter if I'm from Alabama or California? If I'm an orphan or if I have a family? Why do you want to know?"

"It'll take my mind off the itchy mosquito bites," she muttered sarcastically.

"I have anti-itching lotion in my duffel."

He wasn't going to tell her one damn thing about himself. Irritated, hot, sweaty and tired from walking in the noonday sun, she kicked a root in frustration. "You seem to have brought along every necessity in the world. Who taught you to pack?"

She looked up and saw his shoulders twitch with the beginnings of laughter. "Don't tell me, it's classified information."

"Sorry."

He did sound sympathetic, but that only incensed her all the more. He wouldn't share anything about his life with her, and he wouldn't share his body with her, either. She'd never met such a stubborn man, and her frustration boiled over.

"Tell me one thing."

"If I can."

"Do you have any condoms in that pack?"

He halted, turned around and crossed his arms over his chest. "Yes, I do. But we aren't going to use them."

"Of course we aren't. I wouldn't dream of stopping in the middle of the woods, taking off my clothes and making love to a man who can't tell me one thing about himself without violating some...some..."

"Code of ethics?"

"Code of stupidity." She placed her fists on her hips and shot him her best dagger-like glare. "You deserve more than living your life among strangers, risking yourself for people who know nothing about you."

He cocked one supercilious eyebrow. "So you don't want me to try to rescue your brothers?"

"I didn't say that." She would have stomped her foot in a temper tantrum if she hadn't realized how silly she'd look.

"What *are* you saying?"

She smiled at him then, realizing she had been going about this all wrong. Butting heads with such hardheadedness would only give her a headache. So she smiled and bit her bottom lip and watched his eyes focus on her mouth. "I'm saying nothing. Absolutely nothing. The concussion must have rattled my brain. Don't worry about it. I have absolutely no idea what I'm saying."

"Fine." He nodded slowly, but she could see confusion in his expression.

Good. He needn't have everything his way. She was going to give him a little of his own medicine. She knew how to play the silent game. Except she intended to add a few twists, diplomatic twists.

But her plan would have to wait until after the boys were found. She intended to ask Nicholas to make a political request to the Americans to order Hunter to remain in Vashmira until they settled what was between them. She wouldn't have him going off on another mission with so much between them left unsaid and unfinished.

"It looks as if Neve headed back to the car," Hunter told her.

"You think she ran after the explosion and she's waiting for us to return?" Tashya asked.

Hunter held a branch away from her face. "Or she did her job leading us to the cabin and rejoined the kidnappers."

"You don't have much faith in humanity."

"That's how I stay alive."

"But is this how you always want to live?" she asked, curious. If he couldn't tell her about his past, he could certainly tell her about his hopes for the future.

"After my mission here, I've been promised a dream assignment. It's what I've always wanted."

He hadn't given her one detail, but he'd just confirmed her worst suspicions. Unless she could change his mind, he fully intended to move on and leave her behind.

"What happens after your next mission? Don't you ever want a wife and kids?"

"Shh."

He waved her to duck and continued forward. A bullet thudded into the tree close to where her head had just been. Dropping into a crouch behind some bushes, she crawled behind a huge tree.

She realized they'd made it back to the barn and the car. Had he spotted Neve? Who had fired at her?

Tashya peeked from behind the tree to see Hunter leaning over a woman's body. A young woman with long dark hair.

Tashya's stomach clenched into a savage knot. "Neve?"

Chapter Twelve

"She's dead." Hunter removed his fingers from Neve's neck where he'd been searching for a pulse. Gently he closed the nanny's eyelids. "Stay where you are," he ordered Tashya, then dashed to the car, started it and drove straight to her, placing the vehicle between Tashya and the shooter.

Hunter slammed on the brake, shoved open the door, and Tashya dived onto the front seat, slamming the door behind her. Bullets pinged off the car, but Hunter just kept driving. Finally, he tapped her shoulder. "It's safe to sit up now."

He turned to Tashya, concern for her feelings evident. He reached over and put an arm around her shoulder, lending her strength. "We'll call the local police, and they can have the authorities perform an autopsy."

Hunter's voice sounded methodical and cool, almost as if he'd expected to find the nanny dead, but his hand on her shoulder was warm, supportive. And, before he'd dashed to the car, he'd flung his jacket over Neve's body, showing a respect and care that had made Tashya's heart ache.

Tashya hadn't known the nanny well enough to call

her a friend. Like so many people in the palace, Neve had done her job and then gone home to her own life at night. She had truly seemed to love the boys, and they her, making it difficult for Tashya to believe the young woman would have betrayed them.

Even if Neve had been disloyal, she'd been too young to die, barely out of her teenage years. She would never know what it was like to marry and have children of her own. She wouldn't be there to help her mother with a difficult recovery when she came home from the hospital. Nikita and Dimitri would miss her terribly.

Tashya didn't have any tears left. But sadness invaded her bones, settled in her heart and sapped her strength. Hunter didn't seem to have that problem. He drove fast and hard.

"How did Neve die?" Tashya asked.

"From the greenish-blue tinge of her lips, I'm guessing the medical examiner will find a needle mark in the base of her skull and that she died of a poison injection."

Uneasy with the creepy shadows from the trees and the possibility of the killer following, Tashya peered into the forest around them, but saw nothing to indicate that they weren't alone. Still, the bushes in the area were dense and could have hidden a dozen murderers, so could the huge tree trunks.

Hunter spoke with authority. "We have to go on. There's nothing more we could have done for Neve. We have to find the boys."

Weary, sad and full of pain at the loss of a young woman's life, Tashya felt restless in the passenger's seat. While Hunter phoned the local authorities, she went over the events of the last couple of hours—the explosion, the phone call from the kidnapper, Neve's death—but she couldn't make sense of it all.

Hunter drove away from the barn and back down the dirt road. Clouds of dirt rose around them, choking out the sunlight, turning daylight into a ugly dust cloud that encapsulated the car until it reached the paved road leading back to town.

"You think the kidnapper sent someone to murder Neve after she led us to the hut, don't you?" Tashya asked Hunter.

"Yes."

"But since she cooperated and did as they instructed, why did they plan to kill her?"

"Dead people don't talk. I suspect Neve worked for them, but they didn't ever really trust her."

Hunter knew too much about the lack of trust. When Tashya had asked, he hadn't been willing to share one thing about his past with her. In the world he lived in, he was simply protecting himself, but he was also keeping himself at a distance that seemed to grow wider with every mile that passed.

And he unilaterally made decisions, too often not bothering even to explain why. However, she didn't have to let him get away with keeping so many secrets.

Hunter had plugged his cell phone into the recharger the moment he'd started the engine. The tracer sat between the seats almost mocking them since the kidnapper never stayed on the line long enough for the device to pinpoint his location.

She wished staring at the phone would make it ring. The waiting was horrible. She wanted the boys back safe with their mother. She wanted a bath. Tromping through the woods, sweating and rolling in the dust made her feel as if she might never be clean again.

"What are you thinking?" Hunter asked.

"About a bath. A Turkish bath in steamy water. Soaking until the skin on my fingers and toes ripples." She laid her head wearily against the seat. "My father restored the bathhouse at the palace and another at our beach house. He once told me that—"

The cell phone rang. Since Hunter had already connected the tracer, he put the phone on speaker and answered on the first ring.

"Hello?"

A child's voice spoke softly, "Who is this?"

"Dimitri?" Tashya's adrenaline surged at the sound of her little brother's voice.

"Tashya?"

"It's me, sweetie."

"I wanted to call my mother, but I hit the wrong button."

"Dimitri, don't hang up." Hunter pulled over to the shoulder of the road but kept the car running. "You must have hit the redial button. Can you tell us where you are?"

"In the palace. The old—"

The line went dead.

Tashya's heart battered her ribs. "Oh, God, we lost him. Can we call him back?"

"The tracer doesn't have the full number. However, the first three digits match the palace area." Hunter pulled back onto the road and stepped on the gas. "Don't get your hopes up too high."

Was he crazy? Dimitri had just told him where he was. "What are you talking about?"

''The kidnapper might have told him to call us and what to say.''

Anger flared in her that the kidnapper would use a child, possibly threaten Dimitri. She had to restrain her impulse to raise her voice. ''Must you be such a pessimist? Dimitri has always been good at sneaking away from supervision. There's no reason not to think he succeeded again.''

''You have a point. Besides, I've always thought the kidnapper was headquartered at the palace.''

''Because when Sophia called us, her call was traced from her end?''

''Actually there are several reasons. No one saw the kids leave the palace. That's why I asked the guards to search before we left.''

''They would have only searched the renovated section. Why else do you think the boys might be there?''

''When I demanded that the kidnapper let me speak to Dimitri to prove he was alive, I heard several clicks before the final connection. I could be wrong, but the clicks sounded like an extension inside one building rather than from one location to another.''

''You can tell all that from a phone's click?''

He nodded.

''So there's a chance that the boys really are at the palace?'' Tashya turned and stared at Hunter.

''It makes sense. To avoid detection, it would be easier to move them from one part of the palace to another than to sneak them out.''

''But Neve said the boys were in the hut with her.'' Tashya sighed in frustration. ''She lied?''

''Probably. But we had to play it out as if she was telling the truth.''

"All this time that we've been running around in circles, the boys were at the palace?"

"The possibility first crossed my mind again when I saw that the video camera had been looped and that no one had seen the boys being carried out, but I've never been sure. I'm still not sure."

"Then why didn't you ask Nicholas to search again? Because the phones are tapped?" She answered her own question.

"Didn't you tell me that only part of the palace has been renovated?"

"They must be in the old section. I think that was what Dimitri was trying to tell us before he was cut off."

"You mean inside the old walls but not in the renovated palace?"

"There are hundreds of ruined buildings behind the restored palace. Archaeologists from the university are always asking for permission to excavate."

"Look, it's possible Dimitri turned off the phone before the kidnapper caught him. But it's just as likely that the kidnapper knows he called us. They might move the boys again. But I suspect they'll wait until dark. We can be there in less than two hours."

Filled with hope, the weariness slipped away. "You could hide an entire regiment in the old palace and no one would know. The crusaders built the palace inside walls with gates that closed and that could protect an entire city from attack. But in modern times, we've had no need for so much space, never mind the expense of bringing in electrical wiring, plumbing and heating."

"Does Alex have any interest in archeology?"

"I'm afraid not. Why?"

"We need an excuse to explore the ruins."

"No problem. We'll go for a ride. The stables and trails are all around the old section."

"Good. Can you sneak us into the palace so no one will know we're there?"

THE PHONE RANG while they remained a good twenty minutes from the palace. Even as Hunter punched the button to answer, he stepped on the gas pedal.

"Maybe it's Dimitri." Tashya's voice rose with hope.

"Shh." Hunter waited until she stopped talking before pressing the speaker button.

"Meet me at the—" The kidnapper's voice started to make a demand and Hunter hung up the phone.

Her eyes widened at Hunter's action. "Why did you—"

"I'm buying time. Let him think we're having phone trouble."

The phone rang a few more times, but Hunter didn't answer. He weaved in and out of traffic, pushing the limits of the car as well as his physical reaction time, adjusting to the road, other cars and the lights while his mind turned over options.

"The kidnapper is going to demand that we meet him. It's probably not going to be anywhere near the palace." He glanced at Tashya as her face paled. Obviously she understood the problem and the critical ramifications of their ultimate decision.

"Oh, God. We either go after the kids or adhere to the kidnapper's demand."

The phone rang again.

Hunter picked up, said "Hello?" then hung up

again. People usually hung up on other people, not when they themselves were speaking.

"You may be making the kidnapper angry."

"How long until we arrive at the palace?" Hunter asked her. "I can probably stall another few minutes without consequences."

Hunter could read the doubts in her face and her understanding that the next decision they made could be the difference between rescue and disaster. He didn't want to rush Tashya, but as the phone rang again, and again he ignored the ringing, he knew that arriving at a decision quickly was increasingly more critical.

Her voice was strained but calm. "What do you think we should do?"

"Go after the kids. The kidnapper has consistently lied to us. He tried to take us out at the phone booth and again at the hut. Neither time did he appear ready to release the boys in exchange for us."

"But if we don't show at the meeting place, if we don't appear to be cooperating, then he'll have no reason to keep the boys alive."

"We'll have to find them before he can harm them." Hunter sped around a bus, ignored the driver's angry fist raised in the air.

The phone rang again, and he picked it up on the first ring to keep the kidnapper off balance. "We're in the mountains." He lied, knowing that the chain running through Vashmira was hundreds of miles long. "We keep losing the sig—" He cut off the phone again.

Beside him, Tashya looked ill, and Hunter knew he couldn't let her make this decision. If *he* made the wrong choice, it would be better for her to blame him than to live the rest of her life with the knowledge that she'd made a mistake that cost the lives of her brothers.

He could do that for her. It might not be much, but right now that was all he could give. "I'm driving straight to the palace. Can you get us inside without being seen?"

"I think so."

When she didn't protest his decision, a measure of relief swept over him that she trusted him. Trusted him to save the little boys. He only hoped that he could live up to her trust.

When the phone rang again, he let it ring four times, then answered. "Yes?"

"Don't talk," the kidnapper demanded irritably. "Just listen. Go to the ski resort at Lisem. Bottom of the gondola. One hour."

"Two. We can't get there in one."

"One—or the boys die."

Tashya raised her voice to an almost hysterical-sounding scream. "Please, an hour and a half. You've got to give us more time."

"Ninety minutes," the kidnapper agreed and the phone went dead.

"Well done," Hunter told her as he set a timer on his watch to begin a ninety-minute countdown. "You put just the right touch of desperation in your tone."

"I *am* desperate. You haven't seen the old palace. An hour and a half isn't enough time to find the boys without lots more help. There are thousands of rooms. Old passageways. Tunnels. If just the two of us search, it could take weeks."

"Not if we steal your security chief's thermal im-ager."

"His what?"

"It's a device sensitive to body heat. We aim the imager at the old section, and it should show us exactly where the boys are."

"How do you know Ira has one?"

"I overhead one of the guards mention that they'd used it to prevent people from getting lost when Nicholas ordered the tunnels closed."

"Ira keeps his equipment locked up."

"Let me worry about that. You concentrate on getting us into the palace."

"What time is it?" she asked.

"Why?"

"We need 'Uncle' Hadrid on shift." She glanced at Hunter's watch. "If you'd step on the gas, we might make it before he goes home for the day."

"Pedal's already on the floor." Obviously his princess had no fear of speed. Either that or her fear for the children's safety was greater. "Who's Uncle Hadrid?"

"My favorite palace guard. Ever since I was a teenager he'd let me come and go through his gate with a friendly wave, a hearty wink and a warning not to get caught."

Hunter raised an eyebrow. No wonder she'd taken to his kind of life so easily. As a kid she'd had to break rules to escape the palace just to act like a normal adolescent. "You never got caught?"

"Oh, I think my father knew. That's when he made me promise to carry pepper spray in my purse."

"I'm surprised he didn't teach you to shoot a gun."

"He did, but I don't like them much. I wanted to go out so I learned to use a revolver. Father told me that I deserved some freedom. Looking back, I think he had guards follow me at a discrete distance—but at the time, I believed I was on my own. Someday, Nicholas is probably going to have to make the same arrangements for Dimitri and Nikita—if we find them.''

If they found them. A very big *if*.

TASHYA LED HUNTER around to the side gate with two minutes to spare. Of course Hadrid wasn't really a blood uncle but the old guard had always treated her with the same affection as his nieces and nephews. This time was no exception. Since he didn't seem the least bit startled by the prince's presence, she assumed that Alexander had often availed himself of escaping the palace through this very gate.

Once inside, she and Hunter strolled along the towering wall of stone toward the back of the main gatehouse where Ira stored his security equipment. The sun, which had shined almost steadily during the last few days, had disappeared behind an overcast sky, and the gray palace walls seemed more like a prison than a protective structure. Just when her hopes were rising, a damp gray mist of fog shrouded them in gloom.

Tashya whispered to Hunter, although she wasn't sure why, since no one seemed to be around in the gray drizzle. ''There's a back door to the equipment room, but it's always locked.''

Hunter walked beside her. ''Are there guards inside?''

''I don't know. Ira has tightened security.''

Hunter kept walking but slowed his steps. ''I don't suppose I could talk you into waiting here for me?''

She eyed him, sensing by the determined gleam in

his eyes that there were some things he didn't want to say. "We've come this far together..."

"Fine." He shrugged and possessively took her elbow. "I didn't like the idea of leaving you behind anyway."

But she also knew he didn't want her with him. Strange man. Sometimes she wondered if he just yearned to be rid of her altogether, because even though he seemed to care for her, he obviously didn't like having those feelings.

Her speculations ended as Hunter set down his duffel against the stone wall next to the locked back door. He extracted a sharp metal tool, inserted the tip into the lock and picked it open as easily as if he'd possessed the key. No wonder he'd told her not to worry about breaking in.

She followed Hunter inside the darkened room, which smelled of machinery, oil and stale coffee. He flicked on a penlight and headed straight for the area where Ira kept the expensive equipment behind a padlocked, chain-linked fence. Hunter broke through the padlock in less than ten seconds.

The air smelled moldy here, and Tashya kept holding her breath. At any moment she expected someone to come in and find them, but that worry couldn't explain her jumpy nerves. Even if security caught them, the prince and princess had every right to go anywhere inside the palace grounds.

Her heart rate accelerated and her palms broke out with sweat. She couldn't let the time limit get to her. Finding and using the thermal imaging device was critical to rescuing the kids. But she really wanted to run through the ruins, screaming their names, not methodically plot and plan the best method to accomplish her goal.

Steady. Soon, she would be free to gallop her horse over the old palace ruins in search of the boys.

Her eyes adjusted slowly to the darkness. She waited in silence, trying to be patient, as Hunter ran his penlight over the equipment.

"It's not here," he whispered.

"Maybe the military department borrowed the equipment. Ira and Vladimir often share the high-tech stuff."

Hunter pointed the light at a crack in the wall. "That's odd."

"What?"

He leaned into the shelving that housed ammunition and guns and flicked a switch. The entire wall moved back on a silent hinge, leaving them to stare at a wall of television monitors and VCRs that taped activities in various locations inside the palace. The last time she'd toured this room, she hadn't come through the secret entrance, and she wondered why there was a secret entrance as she looked at the screens that revealed the kitchens, the main entryway, several corridors, the ballroom and even some of the private quarters. Did Ira know about the secret entrance? Could someone else have built it and had secretly been watching the comings and goings inside the palace? There were several views of various gates, many interior shots.

A security guard walked inside and snapped on the lights, interrupting her thoughts. Startled by their presence, he frowned. "Highness, I just stepped out for a smoke."

"We're checking on palace security. I don't want

you leaving this room during your shift. If you need a break, call in someone to cover for you. Is that clear?''

"Yes, Highness."

Hunter ignored the guard and scanned the equipment. Something must have caught his gaze because he suddenly focused on several pieces of gear neatly laid out on a table.

Hunter spoke as if Alex had just found his favorite diamond cuff link. "Here's the thermal imager."

She wondered why the thermal imager, the specific equipment they'd needed to find the boys, hadn't been stored in its normal location. Was it simply a coincidence? Had someone borrowed it and forgotten to put it back? Or had Ira anticipated that this piece of equipment would be extremely useful in finding the children and deliberately misplaced it?

Hunter picked up the imager and snapped on a switch. "The battery's fully charged. Let's go."

Hunter didn't bother explaining anything to the security guard, simply closed the door behind them. He slung his duffel over his shoulder and headed around the east wing of the palace toward the stable. Several gardeners noted their passage and greeted them. So did a few merchants who entered and exited the palace through the rear entrance, delivering raw vegetables, fresh fish and tea.

Tashya hoped none of them commented on the prince and princess's presence. She didn't want word to get back to the kidnapper that they were at the palace instead of on their way to the ski gondola as they'd been ordered.

But she could no more stop palace gossip than she could make herself disappear. They didn't have time to disguise their appearance or skulk around in the bushes or wait until dark. They had about an hour left to find her brothers.

Once they reached the familiar stable, her nerves settled a little. A gallop was out of the question in this weather. She requested that her groomsman choose a steady and gentle mare for Hunter and another for herself. She did not want to ride a high-strung animal in the rain over slippery grounds. These mares also had the advantage of being accustomed to the sound of gunfire, part of their training, since her brothers rode them in parades.

While she saddled her horse and the groom performed that chore for Hunter, he sorted through his weapons, slinging an automatic assault rifle over his shoulder. The groom, accustomed to men carrying military weaponry didn't seemed the slightest bit alarmed. As soon as they mounted and rode out of sight, Hunter handed her another automatic pistol, this one small enough to hide in the palm of her hand. Did he expect her to feel safer with two guns?

She took the second weapon from him, checked to make sure it was loaded and the safety was on, praying she wouldn't have to fire it—especially anywhere near the boys. She guided Hunter along a well-worn trail between crumbling ruins of a Byzantine church and an ancient library, and over excavated stone streets that still bore the two-thousand-year-old marks of Roman chariots.

Beside her, Hunter rode with one hand on the reins, his right hand aiming his thermal imager at every structure they passed. She knew he would signal her the moment he spotted anything, but she couldn't help worrying that the kidnappers might spy them first.

Surely, if they were keeping the boys under guard, they would have a lookout.

In their favor was the drizzle that had increased into a light, chilling rain. Perhaps the lookout was huddled under a ledge, his view obstructed. Better yet, he might be snoozing.

Because if the lookout spotted the prince and princess, he might have orders to shoot them out of their saddles.

Chapter Thirteen

Hunter operated the thermal imager with a growing sense of unease. Russian made, the imager didn't have the sensitivity of its Israeli or American counterparts. Nor did it have switches to widen the scope of his search or to home in on the targets. With the maze of tunnels and a labyrinth of crumbling halls, porticos, pavilions, churches, cloisters and corridors that made up the old palace, he wondered if this outmoded heat-sensing device could penetrate the numerous thick stone walls that had been built almost two thousand years ago.

Perhaps they should have obeyed the kidnapper's directive and gone to the gondola at the ski resort. He checked his watch and realized that another twenty minutes had passed, leaving him a mere forty minutes to find the children and rescue them before the kidnapper realized that the prince and princess weren't going to show at the ski slope.

He would have liked to ride faster, but feared he would miss a blip on the screen. Actually he welcomed the drenching downpour since it helped to cool the surrounding stone and would increase the heat differential and thus the prominence of the images.

He'd begun the search in the ruins closest to the palace, figuring that the less back-and-forth activity there was, the less chance the kidnapper would have of being noticed.

But if the kidnapper wanted just to hide out, he might have picked the most remote spot he could find. He considered hurrying to the far end and working his way back to the middle, but a mad dash into danger could get them killed. They couldn't help the kids if they were dead.

They'd just ridden beneath the remains of an arched aqueduct that had once carried water through the old city, when he spotted three blips on the screen. "Hold up."

He stared at the fuzzy images, two small, one much larger and thicker.

Tashya peered over his shoulder. "Looks like two children and an adult."

Suddenly the larger image broke into two. Where there had previously been one rather thick image, there were now two much more slender ones. "The two guards must have been close together and are now exchanging places. If we're lucky, one is the lookout, and he didn't spot us."

"And if we're unlucky?"

"He spotted us, went inside and is calling his boss for orders."

"What makes you think the boss isn't here?"

"He might be. Or he might be near the ski lodge. Or back at the palace." Hunter dismounted and led their mounts into shelter from the rain. "From here, we go in on foot."

Tashya tied their horses's reins to a protruding pipe, then took a moment to wipe the rain from her eyes with the back of her wrist. She didn't say a word about the water running down her collar, soaking her shirt, causing her to shiver and her lips to turn blue.

Hunter checked the time. Thirty minutes.

He slung the thermal imager over his shoulder, set his phone to vibrate instead of ring, and carried his weapon in front of him. "Let's go."

"I'm right behind you."

"Stay close. Try and step where I do. Don't touch anything. There could be booby traps," he reminded her.

"They aren't expecting us," she whispered.

"A good terrorist always has a multitude of backup plans." He stepped into the room, dodged across the ancient street, using the aqueduct's thick pillars for cover. Tashya had taken her weapon from her pocket and ran lightly behind him, matching his stride, keeping up without trouble.

For a moment doubts about bringing her along shook him to his core. His job was to protect a civilian, a princess, a woman, not lead her straight into the villain's lair. He could order her to stay back, but he knew her well enough to realize she wouldn't waste a moment arguing. She'd agree to stay back, and then simply follow him again. It was better to keep her next to him where he could protect her.

At the entrance to a narrow, low building that had long ago lost its roof, he examined the area for tampering. Traps could be hidden almost anywhere, a pressure plate under a rock or a filament of wire at ankle level strung across a doorway. In addition, he listened for sounds of footsteps or breathing, knowing body armor might prevent the heat imager from revealing an enemy gunman. A lookout could hide in innumerable places in these ruins. Hunter breathed deeply, probing the air for the scent of a cigarette, coffee, deodorant or cologne. He smelled nothing but rain, saw nothing but crumbling rocks.

Damning the time limit that didn't allow for the careful advance he would have preferred, Hunter stopped and used the imaging device again. This time, the images were closer, the body outlines more distinct. "Both guards are still with the boys."

Carefully, he used the imager to see if he'd missed other perimeter lookouts, but he picked up no additional signals. The lookout may simply not have gone on watch because of the rain, or maybe the two men felt hidden enough not to need a lookout, or maybe they knew Hunter and Tashya were coming and had placed their priority on keeping the children with them.

"The imager shows two men at opposite ends of a room and the boys between them." Hunter put the imager aside, took the mini microphones out of his pocket, placed one in his ear and handed her the other. He didn't want to leave Tashya alone, but the best way to rescue the boys was for them to surprise the guards from two different directions. And Tashya had made it very clear that the boys's safety must come before her own.

"We need to split up."

Tashya accepted the microphone and placed it in her ear. Her face was pale, her lips grim and tinged with purple. Clearly, she was trying not to shiver.

Hunter picked up a stick and drew a map in the dust. "We're here." He placed an X in the spot. "I want you to go around to this side. Stay hidden until I create some noise. The guard closest to you should turn toward the commotion. That's when you'll have to shoot him. Aim for his chest, that's the biggest target."

She nodded, swallowed hard.

"Princess, the boys will be behind him. Don't shoot unless you have a clear shot."

"I'll be fine," she told him.

She didn't look fine. She'd never killed before and clearly the idea sickened her. She looked scared and cold and slightly green.

"Hey." He tossed away his stick and pulled her face to his. He looked straight into her eyes. "Nothing's going to happen to the woman I love."

Her eyes narrowed, flickered with suspicion and surprise and a tiny hint of gladness and hope. "What did you say?"

"I love you." Then he dipped his head and let his lips claim hers. He held her close, giving her his heat, willing her to believe in him and in herself. He hadn't wanted to put her in a life-or-death position, but he had no choice. Since he had none, he wanted her going into battle with adrenaline surging, alert and confident.

He knew he'd taken her by surprise, thrown her off kilter and momentarily distracted her from her fear for the children. All too soon that fear would re-emerge, but for now, there was simply a man, a woman and a kiss that could have fused metal.

She responded to him with an ardor that made his thoughts spin and his breath ragged. He pulled back a minute or so later, satisfied to see the color returning to her face, the shivers fading.

"Tell me again," she demanded.

"I love you." Then he spun her around, swatted

her very shapely and very firm bottom and sent her on her way. She would never know what it cost him to let her walk into danger, but he put the agony aside. They had two children to rescue.

Before he changed his mind and called her back, Hunter headed off in the opposite direction.

WARMED BY HUNTER'S KISS, Tashya proceeded down a corridor filled with cobwebs, wind-blown leaves and rubble. Hunter confused her, excited her and left her wanting to shake him. Had he told her that he loved her because he didn't expect to see her again? Because either of them could be shot? Or had he declared his love to give her the strength she'd needed to go on?

His declaration had fortified her courage, made her feel worthy and capable of rescuing the boys. She should concentrate on her job, but his declaration of love had come out of nowhere and thrown her for a loop. Then before she could utter one word, he'd kissed her as though they would have no tomorrow.

What was she supposed to think? Or say? First she'd been too cold and stunned to think and after that sizzling kiss she'd felt as though she'd just ridden one of those upside-down roller coasters and had yet to regain her equilibrium.

The man had no business telling her that he loved her when they might not have another hour together. Soon, he would either succeed and his mission would be over and he would leave, or they would both be dead. So why had he told her he loved her? Was it an admission torn from him because he thought they would fail?

A man like Hunter seemed to think only of success.

Yet he was human—all too human, too sexy for her to resist and too mysteriously complicated for her to really understand.

A mouse scurried from its nest, calling her attention back to her progress. Rain pattered down, plopping in puddles that she carefully stepped around to keep her approach silent. She moved slowly down the hallway, her hand on her weapon steady, her heart surging into her throat.

Hunter spoke to her, his voice a mere whisper in her ear receiver. "The boys are lying on the floor, sleeping and out of the direct line of fire."

If the kidnappers had caught Dimitri on the phone they might have given him sleeping pills again. While she didn't want the children to have been medicated, she hoped they wouldn't awaken until they were safe again in their family's arms.

"I'm in position, Princess. Take your time. We have five minutes left."

Only five minutes?

The scent of cigarette smoke warned her that she was close to her target. She kept low and peeked around the next corner. A stocky, gray-haired man in his fifties who wore a military uniform leaned against an open doorway, casually smoking his cigarette. His rifle slanted against the wall within easy reach, but once Hunter started his diversion it would take just a mere second for this soldier to grab his rifle.

"Four minutes." Hunter counted down softly.

From her angle, she couldn't see the boys and hoped that meant they were safe. Even with the sound of rain falling, she feared the soldier might hear her speak.

She withdrew a few steps and spoke to Hunter in

the merest whisper. "I'm three steps away from where I can shoot. He's smoking a cigarette. The rifle's leaning against the wall," she added.

"Change of plans."

Three minutes to go and he wanted to change plans?

Hunter's words jolted her nerves, and she held her breath as she listened to him. "My guy is on the ball. Rifle in hand. You're going to make our distraction."

Oh, damn.

"How?"

"Shoot him."

Damn. Damn. Damn.

"It's the best option. We don't have time to change places. Do it now, Princess, while he's still smoking."

And the rifle wasn't in his hands. He wanted her to shoot an unarmed man.

"Two minutes."

Damn.

Suppose she missed and let Hunter down? She could get him killed.

She didn't belong here. Hunter had no business counting on her. She was a princess—not a sniper, not an assassin. Doubts iced her stomach as she considered whether she could shoot the man.

It was one thing to kill in defense of herself or another. Or during the heat of an attack. But the soldier was just standing there, like an innocent deer in the crosshairs of a scope. Only he wasn't innocent, she reminded herself. If she didn't shoot him, he could kill her little brothers.

"Princess?"

"Okay. I'm going."

Her feet were moving, but her hand couldn't seem to raise the gun, which all of a sudden seemed to weigh more than she could bear. Edging forward to where she would take her shot, she peeked around the corner.

"One minute."

The soldier's cigarette was almost down to the stub. Another puff or two and she would lose her opportunity. She used her other hand to raise the weapon. Still her hands shook.

"Now, Princess."

Tashya pulled the trigger. Her bullet struck the soldier in the shoulder. Everything seemed to move in slow motion.

He dropped his cigarette, screamed in pain. Blood spurted from his shoulder.

Hunter and the other soldier exchanged a flurry of shots. Frozen to the wall, horrified and sick at what she'd done, she told herself she should fire again. She peeked down the corridor. The wounded man she'd shot had picked up his weapon and was rolling for cover, pointing his rifle away from her, toward Hunter. Toward the children.

Without hesitation, she fired again. Missed.

A phone rang—the kidnapper was calling his men, probably to inform them that Tashya and Hunter hadn't arrived at the ski slope on time.

She had to act. Now.

The kidnapper could call in more soldiers. Stop them from rescuing the children. Right now was the best chance they might ever have.

Tashya left the safety of her position behind the wall. At a crouched run, she advanced. She saw one downed soldier. Hunter was hurrying toward the children. The second injured soldier was aiming his rifle at Hunter.

"Get down." She screamed at Hunter and out of the corner of her eye saw him dive toward the children, cover them with his body. At the same time, she fired.

Missed.

The injured solider finally realized that she was behind him. He turned awkwardly, his rifle caught under him. For the moment Hunter and the boys were safe. She was now the target.

A shot rang out. The injured man flopped back to the ground. Hunter had taken him out. The man stared sightlessly at the ceiling. He wouldn't be kidnapping any more innocent children.

Her knees shook, but she managed to stagger to Hunter and the children. She lifted Nikita into her lap, reassured herself he was still breathing and his color looked normal. Hunter opened Dimitri's eye with his fingers and seemed satisfied when the pupil dilated.

"They're going to be okay." He placed an arm across her shoulder. "We're all going to be okay."

So why was she shaking like a leaf on a gusty day? Why did she feel that she'd never be warm again?

Hunter picked up his cell phone and called Nicholas. She didn't listen to his every word as he explained to the king where they were, where the kidnappers expected them to be and that the boys were really safe. Safe. Thanks to Hunter. He'd known exactly what to do and she couldn't have been more grateful.

She hugged her brothers, precious little bundles of mischievous joy, and simply savored holding their sleepy bodies, brushing back their silky hair and breathing in their childish scents. They were alive, unhurt. Tashya looked forward to seeing their mother's face when she arrived.

Tashya didn't have long to wait. The security chief showed first and Ira suggested they carry the boys away from the dead bodies. He and his men would check their identities for clues as to who had given the soldiers their orders. General Vladimir promised to make it a priority.

Meanwhile, Sophia arrived with Major Stephan Cheslav, who had clearly been a help to her during the ordeal of the kidnapping. Tashya had never liked the major since the time he'd made a pass at her, but the way he always seemed to be with Sophia bothered her more.

Although the couple showed up hand in hand, Sophia broke away from Stephan to embrace her sleepy sons, tears of relief and happiness running down her cheeks. After kissing each of her children, she lapsed into huge sobs on Stephan's shoulder.

In the past few days the couple seemed to have grown very close. Under other circumstances, Tashya might have been more suspicious of Stephan's apparent closeness to Sophia, but right now that was difficult with so many of her own uncertain emotions to deal with.

She recalled Hunter's declaration of love.

But now when she wanted to turn to him, he was again acting like Alex, impersonating her brother. However, that wasn't going to last. She would see to it.

STILL IMPERSONATING the prince, Hunter debriefed the security chief. While not surprised to learn that the Vashmiran army didn't fingerprint its soldiers and have an instantaneous computerized identification program, he still believed the wheels of justice could turn faster. Was Ira stalling the investigation? Possibly protecting his friend, General Vladimir? And why had Tashya stiffened when Stephan had held Sophia?

Hunter considered taking his suspicions to King Nicholas, but he didn't have any proof. It was clear that whoever had ordered the kidnapping must have also been responsible for the assassination attempts on the prince and princess. His mission wouldn't be over until he'd found the mastermind. Unfortunately, he'd been forced to kill both soldiers. Although he would have liked the opportunity to question them, he couldn't have risked leaving them alive before he'd made sure the boys were safe.

For the next hour he'd answered the security chief's polite questions, explaining his theory that the kidnappers had wanted to take out Tashya, himself, and the two little boys, then go after the king when security was relaxed. He kept to himself his speculations that the General could easily stage a military coup if the entire royal family were killed. Or that Stephan could marry Sophia and rule Vashmira until her sons were grown. Or that the chief of security could have plotted the entire scheme with Sophia against her husband's first family so her sons would eventually rule. Hunter only had suspicions. He needed proof.

While he'd discussed the children's rescue with Ira, Hunter had noted that Tashya had departed with the royal family. Security began a thorough investigation and the grooms came for the horses. Tashya had accompanied Nicholas and his Secret Service agents, Sophia, Stephan and the boys back to the main palace.

Hunter couldn't prevent the twinge of disappointment over Tashya's failure to wait for him, especially after his declaration of love. She'd never responded to his words—at least not verbally. However, when they had kissed, she'd responded with a passion that had held nothing back.

Eventually he realized he was soaking wet and filthy from his exertions. She'd been cold and dirty, too. No doubt she was as anxious as he was for a hot shower and change of clothes.

Hunter picked up his duffel and trudged back to the palace, concern for Tashya very much on his mind. This was the first time she'd been away from him for more than a few minutes. Now with the boys rescued and the kidnapper's plan to take the prince and princess at the ski gondola foiled, the royal nemesis would undoubtedly come up with a new scheme.

Hunter didn't care how cold or dirty Tashya was, she shouldn't have left, even if she had gone with the king and his Secret Service agents. It was Hunter's job to protect her.

He could have put off answering the security chief's questions, but posing as Alex, he couldn't very well state that the prince could protect her better than the king. Still, he should have found some excuse to have deterred her from returning to the palace with Nicholas.

"Hunter?" Tashya's soft voice came in over his ear receiver. Hunter realized that she had him so rattled over her safety he'd forgotten their two-way radio system was still in place.

"Where are you?" Still annoyed with himself over

his uncharacteristic memory lapse, he replied to her more gruffly than he'd intended.

She seemed to hesitate, then spoke. "I need your help."

He reacted immediately to her soft words, tightening his hold on his duffel and double-timing toward the palace. "Where are you?"

"In the room across from Nicholas's suite."

Hunter pulled from his memory the diagram of the palace layout. He calculated that if no one stopped him, he could enter through the main entrance, skirt around the public areas through a private corridor and meet her in five minutes.

When he'd studied the palace blueprints, he'd assumed that the room where she was waiting for him was part of the king and queen's private quarters, but he must have been mistaken. He considered dropping his duffel to make better time, but he had no idea what kind of help she needed and was reluctant to arrive without his equipment.

He was about to inquire, when he heard a door slamming and an echo. Then splashing?

He came out of the rain and entered the palace, his shoes squeaking wet, his clothes dripping on the mosaic tile floors. He shouldered past two secretaries who tried and failed not to stare at his wet, filthy clothes. "Tashya, are you all right?"

"I'll be fine once you get here." Her voice sounded far from desperate.

"Why do you need me?"

"I'd rather wait until we can talk face-to-face."

Her voice sounded troubled, but calm. As he hurried down the corridor, he decided that if her life was in danger she would have found a way to tell him.

He slowed his steps. He would do her no good if he walked into a trap, but then he recalled that the room had only one door—one entrance, one exit.

He approached cautiously, surprised to find two of the king's Secret Service agents guarding the door. Then it hit him. Tashya wasn't in any immediate danger. It was highly unlikely that those American Secret Service agents were in on the scheme to assassinate the princess and her brother. Tashya was most likely quite safe behind those doors.

This was her way of making him come to her.

Hunter recalled the splashing of water and remembered a second set of blueprints—plumbing and electrical blueprints. In his mind, he overlaid the first set, which held the plans of the room's layout, with the plumbing plans. This room, guarded by Secret Service agents, was the royal bath that their father had renovated.

And Tashya was waiting inside for him. In a Turkish bath. He'd be willing to bet a month's pay she'd dismissed the attendants. She would be alone. Possibly naked.

At the thought, his adrenaline pumped. His princess was tired of waiting for him to make a move. She'd known he wouldn't compromise her and the children's safety with distractions. But with the boys now safe with Sophia and the Secret Service guarding this one door, he could let down his guard. He was free to go to the woman he loved and show her exactly how much she meant to him.

Joy swept away his anxiety. Habit kept him clenching his duffel full of weapons as he nodded at the Secret Service agents and then stepped through the door.

Chapter Fourteen

Tashya had never done anything so bold in her life. After her deception, she half expected Hunter to rush in with his gun in hand. Not for one second did she fear he'd fire the weapon without cause. Hunter was methodical. He always thought before he made a move.

Tashya had planned this seduction with the care of a general. The Secret Service agents outside had orders that the prince and princess were not to be disturbed. She'd ordered finger foods and wine, then told all the servants to leave. With the water in the main pool steaming, a stack of plush towels and fragrant soap on hand, she'd decided that this was the most sensual room in the palace. Hunter wouldn't be able to resist her here where she intended to show him how much she loved him. She'd already washed the grime from her skin by taking a quick shower. Wearing only a towel, she waited impatiently.

Hunter strode through the door. As always, alert and aware of his surroundings, he perused the lush bath area, taking in the indoor garden, the marble likenesses of ancient gods and goddesses painted in rich colors and standing every few paces under the domed skylight before his gaze settled on her. His eyes flared with an intensity that made her breath hitch halfway to her throat. She wanted this man, not just for the moment but for forever.

"Hi, Princess." He set his duffel down by the thickly padded loungers and came to her, his eyes locking with hers. "You said you needed me?"

"Ah, yes." She pointed to a stool. "I need you to sit right there."

"Yes, ma'am." A smile teased his lips but didn't quite break out.

He did as she asked. His eyes were now on the same level as the towel knotted at her breasts. One twist was all that kept him from all of her. But she shoved the delicious thought away. And unbuttoned *his* dirty shirt, revealing his magnificent shoulders, powerful chest and classic washboard abdominal muscles.

Her mouth watered. Her palms itched to explore. Finally she was almost free to touch, to caress, to linger, to show him how much she cared.

She licked her bottom lip with a touch of awe and nerves. "Ever taken a Turkish bath?"

He shook his head and his voice came out low and husky. "Not like this one."

"We have our own version in Vashmira. It's a combination of the best the Romans, the Turks and the Japanese have to offer."

He snagged her around the waist, catching her off guard and lazily tugging her toward him. "Then we won't be breaking tradition if we start with a kiss."

Without waiting for her reply, he tilted back his head and nibbled a path up her neck, nuzzled her ear, shooting exquisite tingles that made her bubble with happiness. Surely he wouldn't be kissing her if he didn't intend to make love to her?

But he *had* kissed her before and then pulled back, leaving her yearning for what she couldn't have. Him. All of him.

As his mouth claimed hers, she vowed this time would be different. For a moment he melted away her doubts with his kiss, took away her qualms and banished any thought of failure.

Somewhere as an afterthought, she knew she was losing control. Not a good idea when she wanted to be the one to push him over the edge, to convince him they belonged together.

She pulled back with a hard gasp for air. Without even taking a moment to catch her breath, she gestured to his slacks. "Take those off."

"Okay." The gleam was still in his eyes and he was watching her now like a hungry man with a feast in front of him. Hungry wasn't good enough. Before she was done, he would be starving. Then she'd feed him the most delicious meal he'd ever tasted.

She picked up a towel and slung it at him, gesturing for him to wrap it around his waist. His marvelous reflexes had him catching it, raising a questioning eyebrow.

"I need to draw some water," was all she said.

While he shucked his slacks, she filled two brass buckets at the tap, but she made no attempt to hide her interest in the lean lines of his muscles. Evenly proportioned, his sculpted body bore several jagged scars. She had the urge to kiss away the old wounds.

Not yet.

She filled both buckets, the first with warm water,

the second with cool, then returned to him. "Close your eyes."

She tipped the warm bucket of water over him, slicking back his thick, dark hair, sluicing his bronzed flesh, appreciating the path the final trickles took while she imagined tracing that same path first with her fingers and then with her tongue.

She drizzled shampoo into her hands and threaded her fingers through his hair. Taking her time, she scrubbed every inch of his scalp. He kept his eyes closed, his head tipped back to keep the soap from his eyes, and she took the opportunity to admire the sharp angles of his cheeks and the stubborn jut of his jaw. Most of all she enjoyed being with him, sharing this moment, hoping for many more romantic baths like this one.

He might have refused to make love to her before, but this time, she would have her way with him, show him how much he meant to her. He'd kept her frustrated for days. But now it was her turn to give him a little of his own back. She didn't intend to just incite his desires. She didn't intend to just elicit another declaration of his love. She wanted him wild and crazy for her. She wanted to be irresistible. She wanted their lovemaking to be so good that he would never leave.

"Mmm." His tone poured over her, rich as Swiss chocolate. "If you tire of being a princess, I could give you a recommendation as a bath attendant," he teased.

In answer, she poured the cool water over him. He didn't even twitch a muscle. The man had the most stubbornly frustrating self-control.

But she was well prepared for stubbornness. She

picked up a sponge and the sandalwood soap. She took one more look at his smooth back and tossed the sponge. Her fingers and palms wouldn't be denied the pleasure of touching him for one moment longer.

She began with her fingers on his neck, appreciating the powerful cords that tapered to his shoulders, slowly soaping his skin, wondering if someday he'd trust her enough to let her shave his strong face—but not today. Her hands were shaking too much.

His skin was warm enough to stoke her own desires. Yet he held as still as a smoking volcano, seemingly unaffected by her ministrations—until she heard his soft grunt of pleasure, which warned her that he might be motionless but he was ready to burn.

However, she wanted spontaneous combustion.

Skirting around the stool, she gave the same care to his chest, lathering the soft T of hair that dusted the taut flesh between his nipples, which narrowed then disappeared into the folds of the towel wrapped at his hips.

She caressed his skin at edge of the towel, then kneeled and began again at his feet. Soaping his toes, his arches, his ankles, she took her time, admiring the muscular cords in his calves. Tentatively, she stroked his thighs. A quiver in a muscle there told her he wasn't as unaffected as he appeared and gave her the courage to go on.

She stood, pulled him to his feet and then, with trembling but determined fingers, removed the towel at his hips.

His erection revealed that he wanted her, but she ignored it and soaped the small of his back and his firm buttocks. Damn but the man had a tight ass. She lingered there, appreciating the tight curves, the flanks that reminded her of her best Thoroughbred stallions.

She ached to press her breasts against his back, and decided there was no reason not to lose her towel. With a flick of her wrist, she released the knot and let the towel pool at her feet. Then she leaned naked into him, sliding against his soapy wet back, reveling in the feel of flesh against flesh, his hard masculinity to her soft femininity.

"Princess…"

"Hmm?" She reached around his waist to soap his groin and sex. When her hands closed around him softly and sensuously, he released a groan of pleasure. She lingered, leaving not one inch of him untouched, taking enjoyment in the rough rasp of his breathing, until finally, he turned to gather her into his arms.

She stepped away, taking her time, allowing him to see her, but his eyes latched onto hers, holding her immobile and allowing her to perceive his need.

Good.

She'd fully intended to delay their ultimate union, to wash the soap from his body and to drag him into the steamy tub for a long soak. She had him captured for the entire afternoon and intended to captivate him, as well.

"You're playing with fire, Princess."

She filled another bucket with water. "This should cool you down."

She wanted him to simmer, then she'd bring him back with a slow burn. She didn't toss the water at him, but trickled it over him slowly, cleansing away the suds, oh, so slowly, while she took every opportunity to brush against him with her bare flesh.

"You're enjoying torturing me, aren't you?" he

asked her, reaching for her waist, allowing her to slip away as she moved around him.

"You're satisfying a need that even I never knew I had," she admitted.

His absolute control had made her bold, had made her hungry to see how far she could push him. She just hadn't realized how his vibrant response would enflame her own desires. She felt like a tightly strung filly, muscles gathered and bunched and about to leap into the unknown. Yet she was eager to experience the runaway emotions, haunted by the knowledge that if she didn't take this jump, she might regret it for the rest of her life. So she gathered up the boldness inside her and used it to please them both.

She needed to know if the spark between them would simply flare and burn out or ignite a fire that could keep her warm for a lifetime. Her heart skipped a beat in anticipation and then settled to a lustful hope.

"You'll be a lot more satisfied before we're done, Princess."

"Oh, I'm counting on it." She playfully picked up a towel, wondering if he'd stand for letting her pat him dry—just for the fun of it—before they took their bath together.

But then she didn't know how much longer she could wait for his touch. It seemed as if she'd been waiting all her life for Hunter to hold her, to caress her, to make love to her. Despite his declaration of love, she feared she didn't mean as much to him as he did to her.

She patted his face dry, and he stood still. Before she could blink, he slipped his arms around her waist and under her knees, lifting her until his lips captured hers once more.

As he carried her, she sensed the decision in him. He was done waiting.

Or so she'd thought.

He seemed in no hurry, keeping his mouth on hers. He carried her toward the bathing pool as if she weighed no more than a feather. She expected him to walk into the pool, but he moved to one of the lounging pallets.

"I can't wait, Princess. If you intend to change your mind—"

"Not a chance."

Gently, he laid her down, reached into his duffel and extracted a silver foil packet. She took it from him, tore it open and carefully unrolled the protection over him. He might not have intended to make love to her this afternoon, but she could have guaranteed he wouldn't fail to protect her.

She tugged him to her, but he didn't budge. Instead he plucked a leaf from a nearby fern and trailed it across her neck and shoulders, shooting prickles of sensation over her.

Frustrated that he wasn't yet using his fingers, she nevertheless sighed in delight. His gentle feathering, the barest caress of the leaf, was only a temporary delay. She would have his hands on her soon.

"You have beautiful skin," he murmured, twirling the fern around her breast, never quite allowing it to stroke her hardening nipples.

As if reading her mind, his tongue replaced the leaf, his lips nipping, a promise of much more to come. She arched her back, seeking more heat, but he simply dipped his head, swirling his tongue lazily over her belly.

He explored all of her, tasted all of her before she demanded that he fill her. She wanted him inside her when she peaked. When he didn't immediately comply, she rolled him to his back and straddled his hips.

She lowered herself onto him slowly, watched his eyes blaze with need, heard his gasp for air, luxuriated in the buck of his hips that told her he wanted to pump into her hard and fast.

She gave him slow and easy. Until he reached between her thighs and taunted her, teased her with slick fingers and an easy touch.

Despite her intentions to go slowly, her hips moved at their own pace, picking up speed. He let her have her way for a while, until with a growl of need he clasped her hips in his hands and thrust into her deep, hard. Fiercely. No holding back.

Blood roared in her ears. She'd wanted to watch his face as he spilled inside her. But the sensations were too primal. Then he was taking her with him over the edge, and she exploded, grasping his shoulders, holding him tight, letting her glorious climax spin her out of control.

When she finally regained some control over her thoughts, she realized that she'd collapsed on top of him. While her breathing still came in harsh pants, she found herself held by his strong arms and cuddled against his chest, his heart thudding against her ear.

And she inexorably knew her own mind. She loved this man. She wanted to spend the rest of her life with him, wanted him more than she desired to remain in Vashmira, wanted him enough to give up her title and follow him wherever he decided to go.

Oh, damn. She'd never expected to feel this way, never realized it would irrevocably change her.

That she could give up her home, her country and her family for Hunter stunned her to the depths of her soul. She hadn't expected her love for him to overwhelm everything she'd set out to accomplish for herself.

If she gave up who and what she was for him today, could she respect herself tomorrow?

Physically satiated, mentally confused, she lifted her head, needing to see the expression in Hunter's eyes. He stared at her as if he'd never seen her before, as if he wanted to hold this memory close to his heart forever.

Still, she was unprepared for his words. ''Marry me, Princess.''

Chapter Fifteen

Hunter hadn't known until this exact moment, as he remained deep inside her, that he was going to propose. But the words seemed right. The sentiment was right. They belonged together.

Yet while his own words stunned him, she looked shocked, scared and very much unprepared to make any kind of life-altering decision.

He eased himself out from under her, sensing that she needed not only some time but some space. Experienced enough to know his own mind, to know that their love was special enough to keep forever, he realized that she had yet to reach the very same conclusion.

Using a faucet and bucket, he rinsed and then returned to her side with a washcloth. As tenderly as if she were a baby, he cleansed away their perspiration, then carried her into the pool, very aware that she had yet to give him an answer.

"What are you thinking?" he asked gently, prepared to counter her every argument.

"I would be willing to live with you in your country, but I can't picture myself just sitting around waiting for you to return from one of your missions—"

She hadn't understood. That she would even consider leaving Vashmira for him floored him, humbled him, and gave him hope that they would one day wed.

"Whoa. Stop. I'm not asking you to move to my country."

She leaned her head against the edge of the marble tub, let her feet float to the surface. "Long-distance marriages don't work. What about your next assignment? Could you request to work in Europe?"

"I can find other work…in Vashmira." Her startled gaze flew to meet his. "Work where I won't be risking my life every day." He paused, then went for the whole ball of wax. "You once asked me what I wanted beyond my next mission and I didn't answer. But now I know. I want children, Princess. Our children. I want to raise them with you. That means being together—every day."

"You would stay here? You wouldn't miss your family and the excitement of your work?"

He shook his head. "Not if I have you. My sisters and parents can visit." He ran a hand through his hair. "I've never taken a mission for the excitement, but out of duty, because my country asked it of me and because I was good at my job. I've done enough. Now, it's someone else's turn."

She could continue her work for women's rights, but what about his work? "What would you do in Vashmira?"

"Reorganize palace security, for starters. Update your military technology. Help bring Vashmira's communications systems into the new millennium. I have an idea or two."

In truth, he was brimming with ideas, with plans, with hope for a new life with the woman he loved.

"I only see one problem," she told him.

"What?"

"Nicholas has always planned for me to make a politically advantageous marriage."

Hunter kissed her on the forehead. "Let me deal with the king."

TASHYA DRESSED IN clean clothes while Hunter continued to soak in the tub. She might be intoxicated with the possibility of marrying Hunter, but she knew better than to let Hunter speak to Nicholas before she warned him. Nicholas didn't like surprises, and she couldn't take the chance that the two strong men wouldn't enter into a power struggle that would dash all her hopes. Her marriage needed to be negotiated delicately. As much as she trusted Hunter, she needed to break the news to Nicholas or he would be hurt.

However, she saw no reason to argue with Hunter when she could simply talk to her brother privately first. She supposed some women might think her actions slightly duplicitous, however most women hadn't grown up in a palace. She understood all too well that politics and Vashmira's well-being governed every move Nicholas made. He'd even accepted an arranged marriage to a stranger to solidify his political ties to the West. Falling in love with his bride had been a bonus.

However, since Nicholas was so much in love with his American bride, he should understand Tashya's feelings for Hunter. But another marriage to an American was not what Nicholas had wanted for her. He'd much prefer that she marry a man from one of their neighboring countries and seal Vashmiran alliances with either Moldova, Turkey or Bulgaria.

When she finished dressing in the changing room, she brought Hunter fresh clothes, which she'd asked a servant to deliver earlier. "There's food and—"

"Where're you going?" He asked the words in a lazy tone, but she couldn't miss the curious look in his eyes.

"To my office. To ask my secretary to make an appointment with Nicholas's secretary for you two to talk." Which was the truth. But she also intended to broach the subject with her brother first.

"Really?" His instinct for rooting out deception never ceased to amaze her, but she didn't give in.

"It's better not to interrupt him during an important meeting. We need his goodwill. It would be better to make an appointment."

While she considered whether she'd protested too much, he considered her explanation, then moved closer to the pool edge. In one swift move, he lifted himself from the water and stood. "Take the Secret Service agents with you. Keep them inside your office and apartment until I get back."

"Okay." Her mouth went dry at the sight of him. If she stayed another second she'd be ripping her clothes off and seducing him again. She tossed a towel to him. "Love you."

And then she fled from the bathing room, but not before she heard him say softly, "I love you, too, Princess."

As she left, she extracted her cell phone from her pants pocket and dialed Nicholas. "I need to talk to you."

Her brother sighed. "I'm in a meeting with General Vladimir, can it wait?"

"As long as we talk before Hunter comes to you."

She practically raced through the doors, then stopped, remembering Hunter's instructions to take the Secret Service agents with her. She covered the phone's speaker with her hand and spoke to the agents. "You two, stay with me."

When neither man answered her, she spun around. Both of the Secret Service men's eyes were dilated, their movements sluggish. Their heads wobbled on their necks and they were either sick or drugged.

Quickly she spoke into the phone. "Nicholas, something's wrong."

"What?"

"The Secret Service agents are drugged."

Before she could say more or return to Hunter, Major Stephan Cheslav and four soldiers rounded the corner.

Oh, God. She had to get to Hunter. Warn him. She took two steps back toward the bath. Didn't dare scream for then Hunter would come running, straight into danger.

Tashya pointed with her phone to the drugged men. "These Secret Service agents have been drugged. Alex is in the bath alone and unprotected. You need—"

Stephan roughly grabbed Tashya's arm, causing her to drop her phone to the floor. General Vladimir's aide pulled out his gun. When he pointed the weapon at her, she realized he wasn't here to help.

And Hunter was alone in the bath. She had to warn him. Or had to go for help.

But Stephan held her so tightly that he bruised her arm. With the major's men aiming their guns at the Secret Service agents and about to shoot, terror socked her hard.

"Don't shoot them here," the major ordered. "Take the agents inside. I want the assassinations to appear as if these agents have shot the prince and princess."

His men grabbed the Secret Service agents and took their weapons. Tashya saw they all wore latex gloves. If the soldiers fired the agents's weapons on Hunter and herself, only the agents' fingerprints would remain on the guns.

Obviously, Stephan had no problem revealing his plan to her since he expected to kill her.

"Why are you doing this?" Tashya demanded, trying to stall for time.

"With you, Alex and Nicholas out of the way, I'll be free to marry Sophia—"

"And be the power behind the throne," she finished. Sophia's children were still too young to rule.

"Hurry," Stephan ordered his men, shoving her toward the bath. "We need to be in and out in two minutes."

Tashya's attempt to stall Stephan hadn't worked, but she had to warn Hunter. Screaming a warning would be her last resort because she doubted she'd get much out before they knocked her unconscious and then she'd be no good to him. Instead she waited for an opportunity.

When Stephan looked over his shoulder to make sure his men had the agents in tow, she took her chance. Ignoring the gun at her back, she stomped on Stephan's foot and immediately realized her mistake. While she didn't fear his shooting her out here, since he'd revealed his intention to drag her inside to stage the scene so it looked as if the Secret Service had done his dirty work, she still needed her foot stomp to be effective. But he wore boots. Hard, leather boots that protected his toes.

She planted her next kick on his shin. Only managed a glancing blow, but it was enough for him to shove her hard toward the bath's front door. With the major blocking her escape down the hallway, going for help was not an option.

So she raced inside the bath, ahead of the men and toward Hunter. Any second she expected to feel a bullet in her back.

But the doors had swung back into her pursuers's faces, gaining her extra precious seconds. Hunter, bare-chested and barefooted had just finished buttoning his slacks.

"Hunter." She slid on the slick marble.

Hunter steadied her, took one look at her face and before she said a word, grabbed her hand, scooped up his weapons and yanked them behind a stone planter.

"How many?" he asked, his calm slowing her panic.

"Five. Stephan—the general's aide—is the traitor. He intends to kill us and make it—"

At the burst of gunshots she stopped talking. Tile chips exploded near her head. Automatically she closed her eyes, then had to force them open.

Hunter pressed a gun into her hand. "Stay down."

Then he squeezed off several shots. She heard a yelp and a hoarse scream of pain. Staying low, she peered around the planter. Two of Stephan's men had taken cover behind the drugged Secret Service agents. Hunter had picked off one soldier. Stephan and the other three soldiers had taken cover behind thick ceramic urns that held potted palms.

Hunter kept firing and tugged her close to him. "Don't move, Princess."

She had to shout over the sound of bullets. "They're trying to surround us."

Surely someone would hear the gunfire and send palace security to investigate. But would help arrive in time?

She and Hunter crouched back to back. "Don't waste your shots, Princess."

He fired and then she asked, "Are we low on ammunition?"

"No, but I don't have time to dig out more rounds for your gun. Make each shot count."

"Okay."

Hunter must have hit another man because for a moment the shooting slowed. Tashya held her gun ready, waiting for one of the soldiers to attack. Afraid to blink in the smoke-filled room, she first spied the gleam of a metal gun, saw fingers pointing the weapon, then the man stuck his head out from behind a column. She fired.

She had no idea whether her shot found its mark, but the man didn't try to shoot back. Gulping, she felt rather than saw Hunter ram another clip into his gun. In the split second he took to reload, two soldiers moved in.

She fired, and they ducked back. Then Hunter was calmly firing and picked them off one by one. That left a single soldier and Stephan unhurt and on the attack.

From above them, the soldier flung himself at Hunter. Somehow the man must have crept up unnoticed into the huge planter during the shooting. The soldier dived at Hunter and the two men rolled, punching, kicking, head butting.

Tashya didn't dare shoot for fear of hitting Hunter. And where was Stephan?

She peeked between the ferns to see him crouching over one of the Secret Service agents. The major was about to shoot the drugged agent.

Ears ringing, Tashya raised her gun. Fired. Her shot struck Stephan in his side. A second shot—one she didn't fire—caught him right between the eyes, killing him where he crouched.

Confused, Tashya looked across the room to see General Vladimir had fired the shot that had killed his aide.

At almost the same moment Hunter took out the soldier, the sound of the man's neck cracking leaving no doubt as to his fate.

Then Nicholas and the general were running over to Tashya. "Are you all right?"

The moment gunfire ceased, Nicholas, followed by protesting Secret Service agents, entered the room.

Hunter reached her side before either the king or the general crossed the room, and she flung herself into his arms. "When Stephan grabbed me, I thought I'd never see you again."

And suddenly Tashya realized that she wasn't acting like Alex's sister, but like Hunter's lover. But with Stephan dead, it no longer mattered.

General Vladimir looked from Hunter to Nicholas and then at Tashya. While the king explained Hunter's impersonation of Alex, she wound her arms around Hunter's neck and kissed him.

She needed to drink in his strength, needed to re-assure herself he was unhurt, needed his arms around her. When Hunter pulled back from their kiss, he made no explanation to her brother.

"I appreciate your showing up to help out." Hunter told the general and the king. "How did you know…"

Nicholas's eyes narrowed with speculation. "Tashya was speaking to me on the phone. I could hear enough of the conversation to understand she was in trouble."

"She was calling *you?*" Hunter asked.

Not her secretary, as she'd told him she was going to do. *Uh-oh.*

Tashya needed a diversion. "Nicholas, how upset is Sophia going to be over Stephan's death? The two of them seemed to have gotten rather close while I was gone."

"She'll be fine. As a matter of fact, last night she asked me to transfer Stephan to another position. Apparently once the children were back, she realized that she didn't have feelings for him. The general and I were discussing his transfer when you called."

Damn him. Nicholas had deliberately circled the conversation right back around to where she hadn't wanted it to go. But she received another reprieve when Ira and his security team arrived and shooed them all out of the bathhouse. However, neither her brother nor Hunter appeared inclined to let her out of their sight until explanations were made.

Nicholas ushered them into his private apartments and Hunter took the opportunity to put on Alex's shirt. The general had stayed behind, leaving Tashya alone with Hunter and Nicholas. Once they arrived in the royal office, Nicholas offered Hunter a drink. He declined.

Nicholas walked around his desk and looked out the window for a moment before turning to face Hunter. "What's on your mind?"

Tashya knew that Nicholas hadn't forgotten her request to speak with him privately before Hunter did. That he would discount her wishes didn't bode well for her. But interrupting would only irritate both men.

Hunter, also, remained on his feet. "I'd like your permission to marry Tashya."

"And if I don't give that permission?"

"Your Majesty, you don't want me to answer that question." Hunter's voice softened, but somehow the words came out with a hint of a threat in them.

Nicholas, she couldn't read at all. However, this might be the most important decision of her life and both men were talking about her future as if she wasn't even there. Tashya simmered with anger, yet held her annoyance in check. She would speak her mind when the time came—but not yet.

Hunter had thrown the ball back in Nicholas's court and her brother thrummed his fingers on the desk, deep in thought. "I'd hoped to strengthen Vashmiran ties to our neighbors with a royal marriage. But I suspect it's too late for that now." Nicholas glared at Hunter.

Unperturbed, Hunter held Nicholas's gaze. "It's much too late."

"My new bride happens to be quite perceptive," Nicholas admitted. "And she believes people in love should marry." Apparently, Queen Ericka had suspected the budding romance and had put in a good word for her countryman, but would that sway Nicholas?

Tashya went to stand next to Hunter. She took his

hand, realizing that Hunter was an excellent negotiator—especially since he wasn't going to take *no* for an answer.

"You'll live in Vashmira?" Nicholas asked, and Tashya knew that her brother had just given in. But she withheld any outward sign of joy, just squeezed Hunter's hand more tightly. She would continue her fight for women's rights, live near her family and marry Hunter, too.

Hunter turned to Tashya then, his look full of love. "We'll live wherever the princess wishes."

Nicholas came around his desk, put one arm around each of them. "I wish you a happy marriage and years of joy."

Tashya hugged her brother. "There's just one more thing."

Nicholas raised his brow. "Yes?"

"Hunter has some ideas to help upgrade our security."

He kissed Tashya on the cheek. "I'd welcome his suggestions." Nicholas turned to Hunter. "In fact, if you'll accept a position in Vashmira, I'd be grateful for your expertise."

Hunter nodded his acceptance.

"I'll call Alex and fill him in." Nicholas shook Hunter's hand and departed, closing the door softly and leaving them alone.

Tashya flung her arms around Hunter's neck and plastered kisses on his lips and neck. "You were brilliant. You stood up to Nicholas with just the right combination of strength and respect." She smoothed her palm down his cheek. "Just exactly what would you have done if Nicholas refused to allow us to marry?"

Hunter flashed her a teasing grin. "I've learned from an expert. I simply would have agreed to do what Nicholas asked—leave Vashmira and forget about you."

"You would have left me?"

"No, Princess, I would have *agreed* to leave you, but then I'd have smuggled you across the border." His glance was mischievous and sexy. "I love you way too much to leave you."

*We hope you enjoyed ROYAL RANSOM,
book two of Susan Kearney's*
THE CROWN AFFAIR.
*Please look for book three,
ROYAL PURSUIT,
(HI #690, 12/02) next month. For a
sneak preview of ROYAL PURSUIT,
turn the page…*

Prologue

"Highness," Prince Alexander's secretary signaled him through the intercom. "King Nicholas is on line four."

Alex hadn't spoken to his brother in weeks for fear that calls from the royal palace to the Vashmiran embassy in Washington, D.C., might be intercepted. Through diplomatic channels, he'd been told to lie low until the person or persons out to assassinate him had been caught.

Anxious over the problems back home, worried about the rest of his family's safety, especially that of his sister Tashya, whose life had also been threatened, Alex immediately picked up the phone. "Is everybody okay?"

"Yes," Nicholas reassured him. "General Vladimir's aide and right-hand man is dead, and Tashya is safe." Alex relaxed his fingers, which had been gripping the phone tight enough to crack the casing. Their father had been assassinated last year, and a few weeks ago, Nicholas, the new king, had become a target. And then the general's aide had gone after Alex and their sister. That the traitor was now dead was excellent news. Alex's interminable hiding could come to an end.

As if reading his thoughts, Nicholas continued, "My chief of palace security is not convinced the danger is over. We think there may be a conspiracy."

"What kind of conspiracy?"

"We don't know. This may be an internal problem or it might come from one of our neighbors."

Vashmira, a new country founded by Alex's father, had broken away from the former Soviet Union and the new king wanted to strengthen ties to the West. Vashmira bordered Moldova, Turkey, Bulgaria and the Black Sea, and its people were a mixture of religions and ethnic groups. Enemies could come from within or without, and clearly this latest enemy had proved deadly and cagey.

Made restless by his confinement inside the half-finished embassy walls, Alex frowned. "Can you be certain our security chief isn't trying to justify his job?"

"You know better. What you don't know is that Tashya is getting married."

"To the toad?" Alex couldn't believe she'd knuckled under to Nicholas's pressure for her to marry the crown prince of Moldova when she clearly detested the man. On the surface, Tashya might seem malleable, but she was an expert at getting her own way and neither Nicholas nor Alex had ever quite figured out how she accomplished it.

"I've agreed to a marriage between her and Hunter, the American we spoke about last week."

"Tashya's happy?"

"She's in love. However, the Moldovan government is not pleased. I wouldn't be surprised if they are behind these assassination attempts. It would be prudent for you to maintain a low profile for a few more days.''

Weary of remaining in hiding, Alex silently groaned and felt compelled to make the offer, ''Maybe I should come home. Attend a few parties…'' He often acted the part of the playboy who didn't take politics seriously, and it was surprising what kind of information he picked up at a jet-set party—while enjoying himself. But his new job of ambassador to the U.S. would allow him to help his country in a different way.

''Stay and open our embassy if you want. Right now we need to strengthen out contacts with the West, take advantage of my marriage and Tashya's engagement to Americans.''

King Nicholas might speak like a crafty politician, but that didn't mean he wasn't totally in love with his new bride. Alex hoped his sister would be just as content.

He hung up the phone, gratified that Nicholas hadn't demanded that he return. Although Alex had traveled extensively through Europe, Northern Africa and parts of Asia, he hadn't been to the United States before. He'd been eagerly awaiting the time when he could leave the Vashmiran embassy to explore, to accept the dozens of diplomatic invitations he would receive, to meet American women and perhaps to take a romantic sail down the Potomac. Nicholas may have suggested that he continue to hide, but now that the immediate crisis was over, Alex refused to remain secluded any longer. Long ago he'd accepted that royalty and politicians were always targets and, while cautionary measures at certain times were prudent, he wouldn't spend a lifetime in hiding.

Alex left his office for his private suite inside the embassy and retreated to his living room, savoring the options that would soon be his. He sat in the most comfortable chair and picked up a book he had been reading, but he couldn't concentrate on it. He wanted to be free. Free to act like a tourist and tour the Smithsonian, enjoy a drink at the Sequoia. Free to explore the Washington Monument, free to taste ice cream from a street vendor, free to enjoy the company of a sensual woman.

Although generalizations could prove dangerous, he often found them to be true. European women had a certain diamond-like sophistication, a je ne sais quoi, a refined style that had been honed for generations and which he'd appreciated with gratitude. In Asia, the women were like pearls, each one precious and polished, tending to the men with a respect founded on rituals.

And American women? He couldn't wait to meet them.

Alex savored the idea of just walking down Massachusetts Avenue and Embassy Row. Most people in this country wouldn't recognize him, and for a few hours he could pretend to be an ordinary citizen out for an afternoon stroll. His bodyguards had long ago learned discretion.

Freedom beckoned. His presence here had been kept a secret from all but a trusted few, and if he remained careful, the ever-vigilant American and European paparazzi might not find him for several days. He intended to make the most of his rare opportunity.

Fiery pain suddenly looped his throat.

Alex jerked upright. Raising his fingers to his neck, he touched a cruel wire that cut off his air and was much too thin to grab. He flung his arms away from his neck, frantically searching for a weapon. His fingers closed on the lamp on his nightstand.

Alex smashed the lamp against the table and shoved the shards into his attacker. The man screamed.

The garrote around Alex's throat loosened; he gasped in air and shouted for his bodyguards. Behind him, the screams of his assailant ceased, but the unmistakable click of a gun hammer being pulled back gave Alex an instant's warning.

A bullet hissed by his ear as he dived through the doorway, rolled to his feet and sprinted down the hall. His suite door was wide open, and in the dim light he spied the bodies of his guards, their necks twisted at odd angles. Dead.

Footsteps and the sound of wood splintering next to his head urged him to leap over the bodies and zigzag down the embassy's corridor. Cursing under his breath, hoping the blood oozing down his neck was from a superficial wound and that the assassin hadn't nicked an artery, Alex bolted into the grand and uncompleted foyer.

He raced through the nearest exit, past more dead guards. His military training had taught him that the first few moments after an attack could be critical to survival. Without a weapon, returning to fight a deadly opponent would be suicidal. As much as he would have preferred to confront his enemy, he wanted to do so from a position of strength.

Run or hide?

He had just seconds to decide. Pounding down the

wide street in the middle of the night, Alex searched for a place to disappear among the dark office buildings and parked vehicles on the block. Seeing nothing promising, he arbitrarily hung a hard right, then a left at the next two intersections.

He told himself things could be worse. He spoke English, was dressed in slacks and a shirt, instead of pajamas, and was wearing shoes. His injury didn't appear severe, although it still stung like hell. He had his wits about him, and he'd seemed to have outrun his attacker.

Unfortunately, he was lost in a strange country. He knew no one here.

He had no identification and no money. But somehow he would manage, he was sure of it.

And then a car turned the corner, its headlights locking onto him like a heat-seeking missile to a hot target.

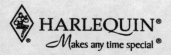

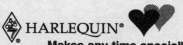

HARLEQUIN®
INTRIGUE®

presents

NIGHTHAWK ISLAND

by award-winning author
RITA HERRON

On an island off the coast of Savannah doctors conduct
top secret research. Delving deep into uncharted
territory, they toy with people's lives. Find out what
mysteries lie beyond the mist this December in

MEMORIES OF MEGAN

A man has memories of passionate nights spent in the arms
of a beautiful widow—a woman he's never met before.
How is this possible? Can they evade the sinister forces
from Nighthawk Island and uncover the truth?

Available wherever Harlequin books are sold!

HARLEQUIN®

Makes any time special®